About the Book

The "Observer's Book of Airliners" provides an invaluable pocket guide to the major types of aircraft used regularly by the World's airlines. Ninety different airliners are described and illustrated (with colour photographs throughout), ranging from the newest products of such giants as Boeing and Airbus to the elderly but still useful classics such as the DC-3 and the Viscount. Here, too, will be found details of types yet to enter service when the book was published, especially a completely new generation of regional airliners that includes the BAe ATP, the DHC Dash-8, the Embraer Brasilia, the Saab-Fairchild 340 and the CAC-100. Important smaller types are included, too, although these have been restricted, in the main, to those used for regularly-scheduled services. Data have been corrected to the beginning of 1983.

About the Authors

William Green, compiler of the *Observer's Book of Aircraft* for 32 years, is internationally known for many works of aviation reference. William Green entered aviation journalism during the early years of World War II, subsequently served with the RAF and resumed aviation writing in 1947. He is currently managing editor of one of the largest circulation European-based aviation journals, *Air International*, and co-editor of *Air Enthusiast* and the *RAF Yearbook*.

Gordon Swanborough has spent virtually the whole of his working life as an aviation journalist and author, since joining Temple Press in 1943 on the staff of *The Aeroplane Spotter*. He is currently editor of *Air International* and co-editor, with William Green, of *Air Enthusiast* and *RAF Yearbook*, three publications that enjoy a world-wide reputation for authority and accuracy in the reporting of contemporary and historical aviation.

The New Observer's Book of

Airliners

William Green
& Gordon Swanborough

with silhouettes by
Dennis Punnett

Frederick Warne

First published 1983
by Frederick Warne (Publishers) Ltd
London, England

ISBN 0 7232 1643 6

Typeset by CCC, printed and bound in
Great Britain by William Clowes (Beccles) Limited,
Beccles and London

INTRODUCTION

THE YEAR 1983, which sees publication of this new "Airliners" title in the Observer's series, is also the 80th anniversary of the first successful flight by a manned, powered, aeroplane. The ability to fly ("like the birds"!) had long been one of man's ambitions, and success had come in a series of hesitant steps: first through the so-called lighter-than-air craft (balloons and airships) that were lifted by heated air or gases such as hydrogen; then with gliders that depended upon the vagaries of wind and weather to remain airborne. It remained for Orville and Wilbur Wright to make the breakthrough with an inspired application of aerodynamic science as then understood, combined with a practical motive power that at last gave the aviator mastery over the elements and gravity.

The Wright Brothers' achievement was one of the most notable scientific advances of the present century; yet even that early success seems insignificant when contrasted with the achievements of aviation as that same century draws towards its close. Leaving aside the field of military aviation, and the whole saga of space exploration that is itself an outgrowth of aviation technology, commercial aviation alone has a breathtaking impact upon the lives of everyone today. It may be true that fewer than one in 10 of the world's population will fly in their lifetime; but more than nine in 10 will have had their lives influenced in some way by the aeroplane through the part it plays in modern commerce.

This volume—which appears in the revised format of the "New Observer's Book" series but is actually the 100th title in the original list—describes and illustrates no fewer than 90 types of aircraft that are, in 1983, engaged in the business of flying passengers, cargo and mail throughout the world—or are in an advanced stage of development for such a rôle. Even so, the list of contents is not complete, for a number of older types are also still flying in small quantities, and a variety of smaller types—and of helicopters, not here included—can be found plying for hire or reward in various parts of the world. The task they perform is largely taken for granted today, but the Wrights would have been truly amazed to see what progress has been made since their first wavering flight at Kitty Hawk on 17 December 1903. Readers, we hope, will find this compilation of data, silhouettes and colour photographs both useful and stimulating.

WG/FGS

INTERNATIONAL CIVIL AIRCRAFT
MARKINGS, BY COUNTRY

Afghanistan	YA	French Overseas	F-O
Albania	ZA	Departments/Pro-	
Algeria	7T	tectorates	
Angola	D2	Gabon	TR
Antigua	VP-LAA/LJZ	Gambia	C5
Argentina	LV	Germany (Federal	D
Australia	VH	Republic)	
Austria	OE	Germany (GDR)	DDR
Bahamas	C6	Ghana	9G
Bahrain	A9	Gibraltar	VR-G
Bangladesh	S2	Greece	SX
Barbados	8P	Grenada	VQ-G
Belgium	OO	Guatemala	TG
Belize	VP-H	Guinea	3X
Benin	TY	Guinea/Bissau	J5
Bermuda	VR-B	Guyana	8R
Bhutan	A5	Haiti	HH
Bolivia	CP	Honduras	HR
Botswana	A2	Hong Kong	VR-H
Brazil	PP & PT	Hungary	HA
British Virgin Islands	VP-LVA/LZZ	Iceland	TF
Brunei	VR-U	India	VT
Bulgaria	LZ	Indonesia	PK
Burma	XY, XZ	Iran	EP
Burundi	9U	Iraq	YI
Cambodia	XU	Ireland	EI, EJ
(Kampuchea)		Israel	4X
Cameroon	TJ	Italy	I
Canada	C	Ivory Coast	TU
Cape Verde Islands	CR-C	Jamaica	6Y
Cayman Islands	VR-C	Japan	JA
Central African	TL	Jordan	JY
Republic		Kampuchea	XU
Chad	TT	(Cambodia)	
Chile	CC	Kenya	5Y
China (People's	B	Kiribati	T3
Republic)		Korea (Democratic	P
Colombia	HK	People's Republic)	
Comoros Republic	D6	Korea (Republic of)	HL
Congo (Brazzaville)	TN	Kuwait	9K
Costa Rica	TI	Laos	RDPL
Cuba	CU	Lebanon	OD
Cyprus	5B	Lesotho	7P
Czechoslovakia	OK	Liberia	EL
Denmark	OY	Libya	5A
Djibouti	J2	Liechtenstein	HB
Dominican Republic	HI	Luxembourg	LX
Ecuador	HC	Madagascar	5R
Egypt	SU	Malawi	7Q
Eire	EI, EJ	Malaysia	9M
El Salvador	YS	Maldive Republic	8Q
Equatorial Guinea	3C	Mali	TZ
Ethiopia	ET	Malta	9H
Falkland Islands	VP-F	Mauritania	5T
Fiji	DQ	Mauritius	3B
Finland	OH	Mexico	XA/XB/XC
France	F	Monaco	3A

Mongolia	HMAY	Sri Lanka	4R
Montserrat	VP-LMA/LUZ	Sudan	ST
Morocco	CN	Surinam	PZ
Mozambique	C9	Swaziland	3D
Namibia	ZS	Sweden	SE
Nauru	C2	Switzerland	HB
Nepal	9N	Syria	YK
Netherlands	PH	Taiwan	B
Netherlands Antilles	PJ	Tanzania	5H
New Zealand	ZK, ZL, ZM	Thailand	HS
Nicaragua	YN	Togo	5V
Niger	5U	Tonga (Kiribati)	T3
Nigeria	5N	Transkei	ZS
Norway	LN	Trinidad & Tobago	9Y
Oman	A40	Tunisia	TS
Pakistan	AP	Turkey	TC
Panama	HP	Turks and Caicos	VQ-T
Papua New Guinea	P2	Islands	
Paraguay	ZP	Tuvalu	T3
Peru	OB	Uganda	5X
Philippines	RP	United Arab Emirates	A6
Poland	SP	United Kingdom	G
Portugal	CS	Upper Volta	XT
Puerto Rico	N	Uruguay	CX
Qatar	A7	USA (and outlying	N
Romania	YR	territories)	
Rwanda	9XR	Vanuatu	H4
St Kitts-Nevis	VP-LKA/LLZ	Venezuela	YV
St Lucia	J6	Vietnam	XV/VN
St Vincent	VP-V	Virgin Islands	VP-LVA/LZZ
Samoa (Western)	5W	(British)	
São Tome Island	S9	Western Samoa	5W
Saudi Arabia	HZ	Yemen (Arab	4W
Senegal	6V	Republic)	
Seychelles	S7	Yemen (People's	7O
Sierra Leone	9L	Democratic	
Singapore	9V	Republic)	
Solomon Islands	H4	Yugoslavia	YU
Somalia	6O	Zaire	9Q
South Africa	ZS, ZT, ZU	Zambia	9J
Soviet Union	CCCP	Zimbabwe	VP-W/Y
Spain	EC		

INTERNATIONAL CIVIL AIRCRAFT MARKINGS, BY DESIGNATOR

AP	Pakistan	JY	Jordan
A2	Botswana	J2	Djibouti
A5	Bhutan	J5	Guinea Bissau
A6	United Arab Emirates	J6	St Lucia
A7	Qatar	LN	Norway
A9	Bahrain	LV	Argentina
A40	Oman/United Arab Emirates	LX	Luxembourg
		LZ	Bulgaria
B	China (People's Republic)	MI	Marshall Islands
		N	USA
B	China/Taiwan (R o C)	OB	Peru
BNMAU	Mongolia	OD	Lebanon
C	Canada	OE	Austria
CC	Chile	OH	Finland
CCCP	Soviet Union	OK	Czechoslovakia
CN	Morocco	OO	Belgium
CP	Bolivia	OY	Denmark
CR-C	Cape Verde Islands	P	Korea
CS	Portugal	PH	Netherlands
CU	Cuba	PJ	Netherlands Antilles
CX	Uruguay	PK	Indonesia
C2	Naura	PP/PT	Brazil
C5	Gambia	PZ	Surinam
C6	Bahamas	P2	Papua New Guinea
C9	Mozambique	RDPL	Laos
D	Federal Republic of Germany	RP	Philippines
		SE	Sweden
DDR	German Democratic Republic	SP	Poland
		ST	Sudan
DO	Fiji	SU	Egypt
D2	Angola	SX	Greece
D6	Comoros Islands	S2	Bangladesh
EC	Spain	S7	Seychelles
EI	Eire	S9	São Tome Island
EL	Liberia	TC	Turkey
EP	Iran	TF	Iceland
ET	Ethiopia	TG	Guatemala
F	France	TI	Costa Rica
F-O	French Overseas Departments/Protectorates	TJ	Cameroon
		TL	Central African Republic
G	Great Britain	TN	Congo Brazzaville
HA	Hungary	TR	Gabon
HB	Switzerland & Liechtenstein	TS	Tunisia
		TT	Chad
HC	Ecuador	TU	Ivory Coast
HH	Haiti	TY	Benin
HI	Dominican Republic	TZ	Mali
HK	Colombia	T3	Kiribati (Tonga)
HL	Republic of Korea	VH	Australia
HP	Panama	VN	Vietnam
HR	Honduras	VP-F	Falkland Islands
HS	Thailand	VP-H	Belize
HZ	Saudi Arabia	VP-LAA/LJZ	Antigua
H4	Solomon Islands (Vanuatu)	VP-LKA/LLZ	St Kitts-Nevis
		VP-LMA/LUZ	Montserrat
I	Italy	VP-LVA/LZZ	British Virgin Islands
JA	Japan	VP-V	St Vincent

8

VP-W/Y	Zimbabwe	5A	Libya
VQ-G	Grenada	5B	Cyprus
VQ-T	Turks & Caicos	5H	Tanzania
	Islands	5N	Nigeria
VR-B	Bermuda	5R	Madagascar
VR-C	Cayman Islands	5T	Mauritania
VR-G	Gibraltar	5U	Niger
VR-H	Hong Kong	5V	Togo
VR-U	Brunei	5W	Western Samoa
VT	India	5X	Uganda
A/B/C	Mexico	5Y	Kenya
XT	Upper Volta	6O	Somalia
XU	Cambodia	6V	Senegal
XY	Burma	6Y	Jamaica
YA	Afghanistan	7O	People's Dem. Rep. of
YI	Iraq		Yemen
YK	Syria	7P	Lesotho
YN	Nicaragua	7Q	Malawi
YR	Romania	7T	Algeria
YS	El Salvador	8P	Barbados
YU	Yugoslavia	8Q	Maldive Republic
YV	Venezuela	8R	Guyana
ZA	Albania	9G	Ghana
ZK	New Zealand	9H	Malta
ZP	Paraguay	9J	Zambia
ZS	South Africa	9K	Kuwait
3A	Monaco	9L	Sierra Leone
3B	Mauritius	9M	Malaysia
3C	Equatorial Guinea	9N	Nepal
3D	Swaziland	9Q	Zaïre
3X	Guinea	9U	Burundi
4R	Sri Lanka	9V	Singapore
4W	Yemen Arab Republic	9XR	Rwanda
4X	Israel	9Y	Trinidad & Tobago

AUTHORS' ACKNOWLEDGEMENT

The authors wish to thank the public relations staffs of the principal manufacturers whose products are represented in this book, for assistance with data and photographs. Grateful acknowledgement is also made to the following individuals for the provision of photographs: R T Broad, Austin Brown, H de Wulf, Andrew March, Peter March, S Peltz and B Pickering/MAP.

AEROSPATIALE CARAVELLE

Country of Origin: France
Type: Short/medium range jet transport.
Power Plant: (Caravelle VI-R): Two 12,600 lb st (5725 kgp) Rolls-Royce Avon 532R or 533R turbojets.
Performance: (Caravelle VI-R): Max cruise, 525 mph (845 km/h) at 25,000 ft (7620 m); best economy cruise, 488 mph (785 km/h); range with max payload, 1,430 mls (2300 km).
Accommodation: Flight crew of two or three and up to 99 passengers five-abreast with offset aisle.
Status: Prototypes first flown on 25 May 1955 and 6 May 1956; certification 2 April 1958; first production Caravelle I flown 18 May 1958 and first service (Air France) flown on 6 May 1959. First flights of later variants: Caravelle IA, 11 February 1960; III, 30 December 1959; VI-N, 10 September 1960; VI-R, 6 February 1961; VII, 29 December 1960; 10A, 31 August 1962; 10B/Super B, 3 March 1964; 10R, 18 January 1965; 11R, 21 April 1967; 12, 29 October 1970. Production ended 1972.
Sales: Production total 282, including three prototypes; 20 Caravelle I; 12 IA; 78 III; 53 VI-N; 56 VI-R; one VII; one 10A; 22 10B; 20 10R; six 11R; 12 Super Caravelle 12.
Notes: Caravelle Mks I, IA, III and VI had same overall dimensions, different engine versions and weights. Caravelle Mks VII, 10, 11 and 12 featured JT8D engines in place of original Rolls-Royce Avons, and the Caravelle 11 and 12 introduced fuselage stretches of 3 ft 0½ in (0.93 m) and 10 ft 7 in (3.21 m) respectively. About 90 Caravelles of assorted type were in airline service in 1983, particularly with charter airlines in Europe and scheduled operators in Africa and South America.

AEROSPATIALE CARAVELLE VI-R

Dimensions: Span 112 ft 6 in (34,30 m); length, 105 ft 0 in (32,01 m); height, 28 ft 7 in (8,72 m); wing area, 1,579 sq ft (146,7 m²).
Weights: Basic operating, 63,175 lb (28 655 kg); max payload 18,080 lb (8 200 kg); max zero fuel, 81,570 lb (37 000 kg); max take-off, 110,230 lb (50 000 kg); max landing, 104,990 lb (47 620 kg).

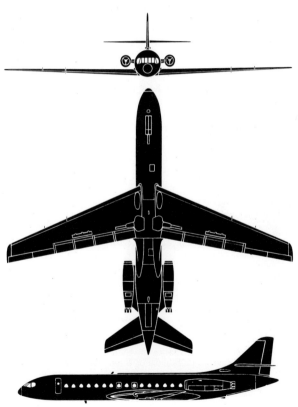

AEROSPATIALE CORVETTE

Country of Origin: France.
Type: Short-range commuter airliner.
Power Plant: Two, 2,310 lb st (1 048 kgp) Pratt & Whitney JT15D-4 turbofans.
Performance: Max cruising speed, 495 mph (796 km/h) at 30,000 ft (9 145 m); economical cruise, 391 mph (630 km/h) at 36,100 ft (11 000 m); range with max payload, 1,022 mls (1 645 km); range with max fuel (including tip tanks), 1,670 mls (2 690 km).
Accommodation: Flight crew of two and up to 14 passengers in individual seats in the cabin, with central aisle.
Status: Prototype SN600 first flown on 16 July 1970; prototypes of SN601 flown on 20 December 1972, 7 March 1973 and 9 November 1973. First full production SN601 flown 12 January 1974, certificated 28 May 1974; first deliveries (Air Alpes) September 1974. Production completed 1977.
Sales: Production total 40; about 12 in airline service, 1983.
Notes: The Corvette was evolved as a joint venture between the Sud and Nord concerns before their merger into Aérospatiale, and was intended as a business twin and to meet the needs of commuter airlines for a small high-performance jet transport. The market for such an aircraft proved to be smaller than expected, however—principally because the sharp rise in fuel costs made the seat-mile costs uncompetitive with turboprop types of similar size. Sales, from stored airframes or through second-hand deals, continued to be made for several years after production ended and the Corvette has found a limited rôle on some low-traffic routes flown by larger European airlines.

AEROSPATIALE SN601 CORVETTE

Dimensions: Span, 42 ft 0 in (12,80 m); span (over tip tanks) 43 ft 5¼ in (13,24 m); length, 45 ft 4 in (13,82 m); height, 13 ft 10 in (4,23 m); wing area, 236.8 sq ft (22,00 m²).
Weights: Operating weight empty, 7,698 lb (3 492 kg); max fuel, 2,928 lb (1 328 kg); max zero fuel, 12,345 lb (5 600 kg); max take-off, 14,550 lb (6 600 kg); max landing, 12,550 lb (5 700 kg).

AEROSPATIALE (NORD) 262 FREGATE

Country of Origin: France.
Type: Short-range turboprop transport.
Power plant (N262A): Two 1,065 shp (794 kW) Turboméca Bastan VIC turboprops.
Performance (N262A): Max cruise, 233 mph (375 km/h); range with max payload (26 passengers), 565 mls (915 km); range with max fuel and 4,343-lb (1 970-kg) payload, 755 mls (1 220 km).
Accommodation: Flight crew of two and up to 29 passengers, three-abreast with offset aisle.
Status: MH-250 prototype flown 20 May 1959; MH-260 prototype flown 29 July 1960; Nord 262 prototype flown 24 December 1962, certificated 16 July 1964. First production (262B) flown 8 July 1964, first 262A flown early 1965, certificated March, entered service August. N262C flown July 1968 and certificated 24 December 1970. Mohawk 298 conversion flown 7 January 1975, certificated 19 October 1976. Production completed 1975.
Sales: Production total 110, including four N262B, 67 N262A and military orders for N262D Frégate.
Notes: The Nord 262 design was based on the original unpressurized Super Broussard project of the Max Holste company, which built one piston-engined MH-250 and a prototype plus 10 pre-production MH-260s with Bastan turboprops. Nord developed a pressurized circular-section fuselage for the N262, built in four variants during which time the company merged with Sud to form Aérospatiale. In the USA, nine N262s were converted to Mohawk 298 standard with PT6A-45 engines and systems improvements, taking their designation from the FAR Part 298 airworthiness regulations then applicable to commuter aircraft.

14

AEROSPATIALE (NORD) 262A

Dimensions: Span, 71 ft 10 in (21,90 m); length, 63 ft 3 in (19,28 m); height, 20 ft 4 in (6,21 m); wing area, 592 sq ft (55,0 m²).

Weights: Basic operating, 15,496 lb (7 209 kg); max payload, 7,209 lb (3 270 kg); max zero fuel, 22,710 lb (10 300 kg); max take-off, 23,369 lb (10 600 kg); max landing, 22,710 lb (10 300 kg).

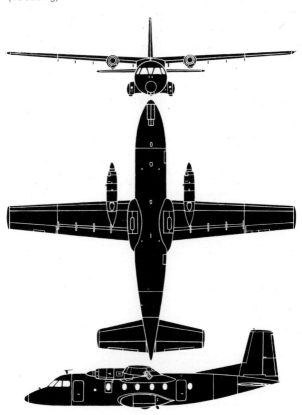

AEROSPATIALE/AERITALIA ATR 42

Countries of Origin: France and Italy.
Type: Regional airliner.
Power Plant: Two flat-rated 1,800 shp (1342 kW) Pratt & Whitney PW120-2 turboprops.
Performance (ATR 42-100): Max cruise, 319 mph (513 km/h) at 20,000 ft (6 095 m); long-range cruise, 286 mph (460 km/h) at 25,000 ft (7 620 m); max payload range (42 passengers), 1,187 mls (1 910 km) at cost econ cruise.
Accommodation: Flight crew and (-100) 42 passengers at 32-in (81-cm) pitch, or (-200) 49 passengers at 30-in (76-cm) pitch four-abreast with central aisle.
Status: Two prototypes under construction with initial flight tests scheduled for August and October 1984 respectively. Certification planned for July-August 1985, with initial customer deliveries last quarter of that year.
Orders: Thirty-nine (plus 14 options) to early 1983. Customers include Ransome (6), Command (3), Finnair (5), Wright (8), Air Littoral (2), Aerocesar (2), Air Caledonie (2), Aliqiulia (2) and Cimber Air (3).
Notes: Collaborative programme for Avions de Transport Regional (hence ATR) between Aérospatiale (France) and Aeritalia (Italy), with final assembly by former. The ATR 42-100 and -200 have same overall dimensions but latter operates at higher gross weight, to carry bigger passenger payload in high-density layout. ATR 42-XX is proposed stretched version for 54-58 passengers, together with ATR 42F freighter and ATR 42QC quick-change versions. Military versions, if developed, are to be assembled by Aeritalia.

AEROSPATIALE/AERITALIA ATR 42

Dimensions: Span, 80 ft 7⅓ in (24,57 m); length, 74 ft 5¾ in (22,70 m); height, 24 ft 10⅘ in (7,59 m); wing area, 586.65 sq ft (54,50 m²).

Weights: Operational empty (-100), 20,495 lb (9 295 kg), (-200), 20,580 lb (9 335 kg); max payload (-100), 8,157 lb (3 700 kg); max zero fuel (-100), 31,096 lb (14 105 kg); max take-off (-100), 32,440 lb (14 715 kg), (-200), 34,280 lb (15 550 kg); max landing (-100), 31,791 lb (14 420 kg).

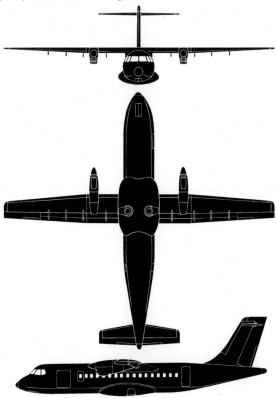

AEROSPATIALE/BAE CONCORDE

Country of Origin: United Kingdom and France.
Type: Medium-range supersonic transport.
Power Plant: Four 38,050 lb st (17 260 kgp) Rolls-Royce (Bristol)/SNECMA Olympus 593 reheated turbojets.
Performance: Max cruise, 1,336 mph (2 150 km/h) at 60,000 ft (18 300 m); range with max payload, 3,050 mls (4 900 km); range with max fuel, 4,490 mls (7 215 km).
Accommodation: Flight crew of three and 128 passengers four abreast with central aisle at 34-in (86-cm) pitch; maximum, 144.
Status: Prototypes 001 and 002 first flown on 2 March 1969 (Toulouse) and 9 April 1969 (Filton); pre-production 01 and 02 first flown 17 December 1971 (Toulouse) and 10 January 1973 (Filton). First two production Concordes flown 6 December 1973 (Toulouse) and 13 February 1974 (Filton). Certification 13 October 1975 (France) and 5 December 1975 (UK); first revenue services 21 January 1976 (Air France and UK). Last production aircraft flown 26 December 1978 (Toulouse) and 20 April 1979 (Filton). Production completed.
Sales: Seven each to Air France and British Airways; first two production aircraft not brought up to full delivery standard.
Notes: Concorde is to date the only supersonic transport successfully put into airline service, although its operation has to be subsidized by British and French governments. Services have been flown on routes to the Middle and Far East and across the South Atlantic, but by 1983 the London and Paris routes to New York and Washington were the only ones flown regularly by the two airlines, traffic potential on the other routes having proved too low for economic operation.

AEROSPATIALE/BAE CONCORDE

Dimensions: Span, 83 ft 10 in (25,56 m); length, 203 ft 9 in (62,1 m); height, 37 ft 5 in (11,40 m); wing area, 3,856 sq ft (358,25 m²).

Weights: Operating empty, 189,400 lb (85 900 kg); max payload, 28,000 lb (12 700 kg); max zero fuel, 203,000 lb (92 080 kg); max take-off, 408,000 lb (185 070 kg); max landing, 245,000 lb (111 130 kg).

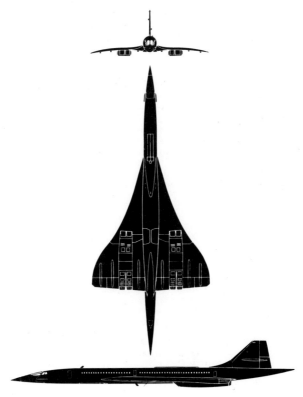

AIRBUS A300

Country of Origin: International.
Type: Short-to-medium range large capacity transport.
Power Plant: Two 52,500 lb st (23 815 kgp) General Electric CF6-50C2 or 53,000 lb st (24 040 kgp) Pratt & Whitney JT9D-59A1 turbofans.
Performance (A300B4-200): Max. cruising speed, 552 mph (889 km/h) at 31,000 ft (9 450 m); long-range cruise, 530 mph (854 km/h) at 33,000 ft (10 060 m); range with max payload (typical reserves), 1,950 mls (3 140 km); range with max fuel, 3,400 mls (5 470 km).
Accommodation: Flight crew of three or (with FFCC) two; typical mixed-class seating for 270; max high density, 336.
Status: A300B1 prototypes flown on 28 October 1972 and 5 February 1973. First B2 flown 28 June 1973; certification, 15 March 1974; entry into service (Air France) 23 May 1974. First B4 flown 26 December 1974; first with JT9D engines flown 28 April 1979; first with FFCC flown 6 October 1981.
Sales: 248 firm orders and about 50 options; 200 delivered.
Notes: The A300 is manufactured by a consortium of Aérospatiale (France), Deutsche Airbus (Germany) and British Aerospace (UK), with small shares held by Fokker (Netherlands) and CASA (Spain). Original A300B2 is now designated A300B2-100; the B2-200 is a "hot and high" version. The heavier A300B4-100 is longer-range version. B4-200 has further weight increase and a300-600 for 1984 deliveries has redesigned rear fuselage. The A300C4 has a side-loading cargo door. The Forward Facing Crew Compartment (FFCC) allows two-pilot operation, with all necessary instruments and controls on the front panels and consoles.

AIRBUS A300B4-200

Dimensions: Span, 147 ft 1½ in (44,84 m); length overall, 175 ft 11 in (53,62 m); height overall, 54 ft 2 in (16,53 m); wing area, 2,799 sq ft (260,0 m²).

Weights: Typical operating weight empty, 194,520 lb (88 200 kg); max payload, 78,900 lb (35 800 kg); max usable fuel, 108,030 lb (49 000 kg); max zero fuel, 273,370 lb (124 000 kg); max take-off, 347,230 lb (151 500 kg); max landing, 295,420 lb (134 000 kg).

AIRBUS A310

Country of Origin: International.
Type: Short-to-medium range jet transport.
Power Plant: Two 48,000 lb st (21 800 kgp) General Electric CF6-80A1 or Pratt & Whitney JT9D-7R4D1 turbofans.
Performance: Max cruise, 553 mph (891 km/h) at 31,000 ft (9 450 m); long-range cruise, 539 mph (867 km/h) at 33,000 ft (10 060 m); range with max payload, over 1,450 mls (2 335 km); range with 210 passengers, over 3,200 mls (5 150 km).
Accommodation: Flight crew of two (or three) and up to 262 passengers eight-abreast at 30-in (76-cm) pitch; typical mixed class, 20F plus 200Y.
Status: Three A310 development aircraft flown on 3 April, 13 May and 5 August 1982, comprising two -220 with JT9D engines and one -200 with CF6 engines. Certification, March 1983, followed by simultaneous service introduction by Swissair and Lufthansa. Production rate, A310 and A300 combined, eight a month by 1984.
Sales: 102 firm orders plus 90 options.
Notes: A310 is a reduced-capacity derivative of the A300, featuring a shortened fuselage, brand-new wing, updated systems and application of new materials where suitable. Basic aircraft, for which data appear here, is the A310-200 (CF6 engines) or -220 (JT9D engines); higher weight options of these are also on offer. In 1986, Airbus expects to introduce the A310-300 with an extra 15,430 lb (7 000 kg) of fuel in the tailplane to increase the range, and a maximum take-off weight of 328,490 lb (149 000 kg). Seventeen airlines have ordered A310s, in various of the -200/-220 options, up to the beginning of 1983.

AIRBUS A310-200

Dimensions: Span, 144 ft 0 in (43,90 m); length, 153 ft 1 in (46,66 m); height, 51 ft 10 in (15,80 m); wing area, 2,357.3 sq ft (219 m²).

Weights: Operating weight empty, 175,863 lb (79 770 kg); max payload (structural limit), 69,947 lb (31 730 kg); max fuel load, 94,800 lb (43 000 kg); max zero fuel, 245,810 lb (111 500 kg); max take-off, 291,010 lb (132 000 kg); max landing, 267,860 lb (212 500 kg).

ANTONOV AN-12

Country of Origin: Soviet Union.
Type: Medium range freighter.
Power Plant: Four 4,000 ehp (2 983 kW) Ivchenko AI-20K turboprops.
Performance: Max cruising speed, 416 mph (670 km/h); range with max payload, 2,236 mls (3 600 km); range with max fuel, 3,540 mls (5 700 km).
Accommodation: Flight crew of five (two pilots, radio operator, flight engineer and navigator). Normally operates only as a freighter, with a pressurized compartment for 14 passengers; space provision for up to 100 passengers.
Status: An-10 first flown March 1957 and entered service with Aeroflot July 1959, followed by An-10A in February 1960. An-12 first flown 1958 (approx) and entered military service in 1959. Out of production.
Sales: Between 800 and 900 An-12s built (for all purposes, including military). About 60 in Aeroflot service 1982.
Notes: The An-12 was evolved to meet specific Soviet needs for a military transport, based on the An-10 which was one of the first turboprop-powered airliners put into service by Aeroflot. Of generally similar appearance to the An-10 (which is now out of service), the An-12 had a redesigned fuselage with rear-loading ramp, and provision for a tail gun target, sometimes faired over. Most of those built have gone into military service, but a sizable number is operated in "civil" guise by Aeroflot for freight carrying and others supplied to foreign governments similarly operate on quasi-commercial duties, carrying freight and personnel on international journeys.

ANTONOV AN-12

Dimensions: Span, 124 ft 8 in (38,00 m); length, 108 ft 7¼ in (33,10 m); height, 34 ft 6½ in (10,53 m); wing area 1,286 sq ft (119,5 m²).

Weights (military freighter); Empty, about 61,730 lb (28 000 kg); max payload, 44,090 lb (20 000 kg); normal take-off, 121,475 lb (55 100 kg); max take-off, 134,480 lb (61 000 kg).

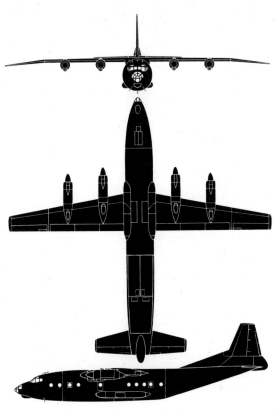

ANTONOV AN-22

Country of Origin: Soviet Union.
Type: Long-range military and commercial freighter.
Power Plant: Four 15,000 shp (11 186 kW) Kuznetsov NK-12MA turboprops.
Performance: Max level speed, 460 mph (740 km/h); range with max payload, 3,100 mls (5 000 km); range with max fuel, carrying a payload of 99,200 lb (45 000 kg), 6,800 mls (10 950 km).
Accommodation: Flight crew of five or six, including two pilots, flight engineer, navigator and communications engineer. Standard layout includes a compartment for 28–29 passengers immediately behind the flight deck.
Status: Prototype first flown on 27 February 1965. Pre-production aircraft used on Aeroflot proving flights 1967. Production completed 1974, total built for all rôles (military and civil) believed to be less than 100.
Sales: No commercial sales or exports; used only by Aeroflot and Soviet military services.
Notes: The An-22, named Antheus, was developed to meet Soviet needs for a long-range transport with the capability of lifting outsize loads, both military and civil. Although approximately 50 An-22s are known to have operated in Aeroflot markings, these have frequently been engaged in ferrying military supplies and personnel around the world, the use of "civil" aircraft in such cases facilitating overflights and transits through foreign countries. The extent to which the An-22 is used in a non-military rôle within the Soviet Union is not known, although its ability to carry such bulky items as earth-moving equipment and oil drilling gear is undoubtably valuable.

ANTONOV AN-22

Dimensions: Span, 211 ft 4 in (64,40 m); length, approximately 190 ft 0 in (57,92 m); height, 41 ft 1½ in (12,53 m); wing area, 3,713 sq ft (345 m²).

Weights: Typical empty, equipped, 251,325 lb (114 000 kg); max payload, 176,350 lb (80 000 kg); max fuel load, 94,800 lb (43 000 kg); max take-off, 551,160 lb (250 000 kg).

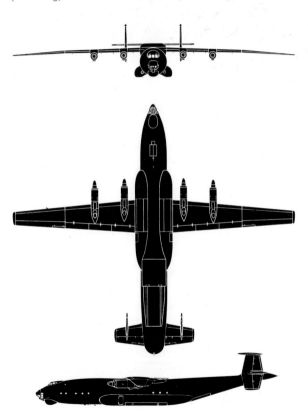

ANTONOV AN-24 AND AN-30

Country of Origin: Soviet Union.
Type: Regional and special duty transport.
Power Plant: Two (An-24V) 2,530 ehp (1 887 kW) Ivchenko AI-24A or (An-26, An-30) 2,820 ehp (2 103 kW) AI-24VT turboprops.
Performance (An-24V): Max cruise, 310 mph (498 km/h); best-range cruise, 280 mph (450 km/h) at 19,700 ft (6 000 m); range with max payload, 341 mls (550 km); range with max fuel, 1,490 mls (2 400 km).
Accommodation: Flight crew of up to five (two pilots, flight engineer, navigator and radio operator), but normally three for passenger-carrying flights. Up to 50 passengers, four abreast.
Status: An-24 prototype first flown April 1960. Service use (by Aeroflot) began in September 1963. Production completed.
Sales: Production total over 1,000 An-24s in all versions, primarily for Aeroflot and export to airlines of all Communist Bloc countries in East Europe and to Air Guinee, Air Mali, Cubana, CAAC in China, Egyptair, Iraqi Airways, etc.
Notes: The An-24 was the first Soviet transport to apply turboprop power for short-haul operations and proved among the most successful, remaining in production for some 15 years. Original basic An-24 was followed by improved An-24V; An-24T was a specialized freighter, and An-24RT and improved An-24RV had an auxiliary turbojet in the starboard nacelle to boost take-off. An-24P was developed for fire fighting and the An-30, which appeared in 1973, has a new front fuselage and was equipped for air survey and map-making. The An-26, with a rear-loading ramp, was developed and produced primarily for military use, as was the An-32 with 5,180 ehp (3 862 kW) Ivchenko AI-20M engines.

ANTONOV AN-24V

Dimensions: Span, 95 ft 9½ in (29,20 m); length, 77 ft 2½ in (23,53 m); height, 27 ft 3½ in (8,32 m); wing area, 807.1 sq ft (74,98 m²).

Weights: Empty equipped, 29,320 lb (13 300 kg); max payload, 12,125 lb (5 500 kg); max fuel, 10,494 lb (4 760 kg); max take-off and landing, 46,300 lb (21 000 kg).

ANTONOV AN-28

Country of Origin: Soviet Union/Poland.
Type: Light general purpose transport.
Power Plant: Two 960 shp (716 kW) Polish-built Glushenkov TVD-10B (PZL-10W) turboprops.
Performance: Max cruising speed, 217 mph (350 km/h); economical cruising speed, 186 mph (300 km/h); range with max payload (20 passengers), 317 mls (510 km); range with max fuel, 801 mls (1 290 km).
Accommodation: Flight crew of one or two; typical seating for 15 passengers three-abreast at 28-in (72-cm) pitch with offset aisle, or maximum high-density seating for 20.
Status: Prototype An-28 first flown in Soviet Union September 1969 (with TVD-850 engines). Pre-production An-28 first flown April 1975 after being re-engined with TVD-10Bs. First production aircraft flown in Poland, 1982.
Sales: Soviet Union has stated a requirement for 1,200.
Notes: The An-28 was selected in the late 'seventies. after a "fly-off" against the Beriev Be-30, to meet Soviet requirements for a light general utility aircraft that could supplement or replace the many hundreds of An 2s and An-14s operating as transports. The prototype was at first known as the An-14M and it shares with the An-14 a high-wing layout with twin fins and rudders, but differs in having a much-enlarged fuselage and turboprop engines. The latter were at first TVD-850s but the more powerful TVD-10Bs have been adopted for the production An-28. The PZL Mielec factory in Poland has sole responsibility for producing the An-28, initially to meet Soviet requirements reported to run into many hundreds of aircraft.

ANTONOV AN-28

Dimensions: Span, 72 ft 4½ in (22,6 m); length, 42 ft 7 in (12,98 m); height, 15 ft 1 in (4,60 m); wing area, 433.6 sq ft (40,28 m²).
Weights: Empty, about 7,716 lb (3 500 kg); max payload, 3,750 lb (1 700 kg); max take-off, 13,450 lb (6 100 kg).

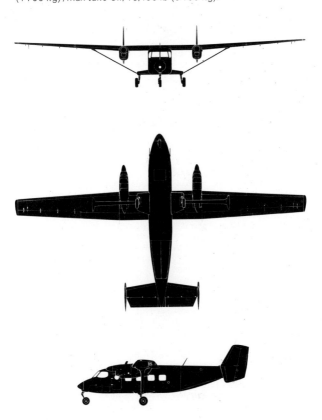

BEECHCRAFT COMMUTER C99

Country of Origin: USA.

Type: Commuter airliner.

Power Plant: Two Pratt & Whitney PT6A-36 turboprops, flat-rated to 715 shp (533 kW) each.

Performance: Max cruise, 286 mph (461 km/h) at 10,000 ft (3050 m); long range cruise, 236 mph (380 km/h) at 10,000 ft (3050 m); range with max payload, 622 mls (1000 km).

Accommodation: Flight crew of one or two and up to 15 passengers at 28/32-in (71/81-cm) pitch, two abreast with central aisle.

Status: Prototype (as a long-fuselage Queen Air) first flown December 1965, and (with PT6A-20 turboprops) in July 1966. Certification of Beech Model 99 on 2 May 1968. Improved Commuter C99 first flown 20 June 1980 with certification July 1981. First C99 customer deliveries 30 July 1981. Production rate three a month in 1982.

Sales: Total of 164 Beech 99 and 99A built. About 35 C99 ordered by late 1982, of which 25 delivered. Early customers for the C99 include Christman Air Systems, Sunbird Airlines and Wings West.

Notes: The Beech 99 was evolved from the Queen Air, from which it differed primarily in having a longer fuselage and turboprop engines, and was intended primarily for third-level airline use. Production was stopped in 1975, but the basic design was upgraded in 1979, with more powerful engines and other changes, to allow Beech to re-enter the commuter airline market; sales began well but were suffering in 1982/83 from the effects of the general business recession.

BEECHCRAFT COMMUTER C99

Dimensions: Span, 45 ft 10½ in (13,90 m); length, 44 ft 6¾ in (13,58 m); height, 14 ft 4½ in (4,38 m); wing area, 179.7 sq ft (25,99 m²).

Weights: Operational empty, 6,397 lb (2 902 kg); max payload, 3,250 lb (1 474 kg); max take-off, 11,300 lb (5 126 kg); max landing, 11,300 lb (5 126 kg).

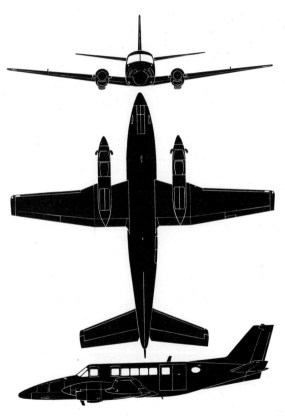

BEECHCRAFT AIRLINER 1900

Country of Origin: USA.

Type: Regional airliner.

Power Plant: Two 1,000 shp (746 kW) Pratt & Whitney PT6A-65B turboprops.

Performance: Max cruise, 303 mph (487 km/h) at 10,000 ft (3 050 m); long-range cruise, 250 mph (402 km/h) at 10,000 ft (3 050 m); max payload range, 637 mls (1 028 km) at cost econ cruise; max fuel range, over 980 mls (1 577 km).

Accommodation: Flight crew of two and up to 19 passengers at 30-in (76-cm) pitch in individual seats with central aisle.

Status: First of three flying prototypes commenced flight test 3 September 1982; certification and first deliveries scheduled for the fourth quarter of 1983.

Sales: No total announced; one early customer for two aircraft is Wings West.

Notes: Beech Aircraft is developing the Airliner 1900 as part of its commitment to re-enter this part of the market, after stopping production of the Beech 99 in 1975. Two versions of the Super King Air 200 were studied—the Model 1300 with the standard fuselage and the 1900 with lengthened fuselage and uprated engines; the latter only has proceeded and there are plans to offer the same fuselage length for corporate use as the Model 1200. Flight testing of the PT6A-65 engines for the Airliner 1900 began on 30 April 1981 in a Super King Air test-bed, and wind tunnel testing of the aircraft configuration led to "tail-ets" on the tailplane tips, "stabilons" on the lower rear fuselage and vortex generators at the wing leading edge/fuselage junction, as shown in the accompanying illustrations.

BEECHCRAFT AIRLINER 1900

Dimensions: Span, 54 ft 6 in (16,61 m); length, 57 ft 10 in (17,63 m); height, 14 ft 10¾ in (4,53 m); wing area, 303 sq ft (28,16 m²).

Weights: Standard empty weight, 8,500 lb (3 856 kg); max payload, 4,000 lb (1 815 kg); max take-off, 15,245 lb (6 915 kg); max landing, 15,245 lb (6 915 kg); max zero fuel, 12,500 lb (5 670 kg).

BOEING 707 -120, 720

Country of Origin: USA.

Type: Medium-range jet transport.

Power Plant: Four 17,000 lb st (7 718 kgp) Pratt & Whitney JT3D-1 or 18,000 lb st (8 165 kgp) JT3D-3 turbofans.

Performance (720B): Max cruising speed, 608 mph (978 km/h) at 25,000 ft (7 620 m); best economy cruise, 533 mph (858 km/h); range with max payload (no reserve fuel allowance), 4,155 mls (6 690 km); range with max fuel (no reserve fuel allowance), 5,720 mls (9 205 km).

Accommodation: Flight crew of three or four and up to 167 passengers six-abreast with central aisle, at 30-in (76-cm) pitch.

Status: Prototype Boeing jetliner (the "Dash-80") flown 15 July 1954; first production 707-120 flown 20 December 1957; certification 23 September 1958; entered service (Pan American) 26 October 1958. First 707-220 flown 11 June 1959; certification 5 November 1959, entered service (Braniff) 20 December 1959. First 707-120B flown 22 June 1960, certificated 1 March 1961, entered service (American Airlines) 12 March 1961. First Boeing 720 flown 23 November 1959, certificated 30 June 1960, entered service (United) 5 July 1960. First Boeing 720B flown 6 October 1960, certificated 3 March 1961, entered service (American) 12 March 1961.

Sales: Production totals, 60 Model 707-120 and 78 -120B (plus -120s converted); 65 Model 720 and 89 720B (plus 720s converted); five 707-220.

Notes: Original Boeing 707-120s and 720s, which were powered by JT3C turbojets had virtually disappeared from airline service by 1983.

BOEING 720B

Dimensions: Span, 130 ft 10 in (39,87 m); length, 136 ft 9 in (41,68 m); height, 41 ft 7 in (12,67 m); wing area, 2,521 sq ft (234,2 m²).

Weights: Basic operaring weight, 115,000 lb (52 163 kg); max payload, 41,000 lb (18 600 kg); max fuel weight, 99,504 lb (45 134 kg); max zero fuel, 156,000 lb (70 762 kg); max take-off, 234,000 lb (106 140 kg); max landing, 175,000 lb (79 380 kg).

BOEING 707-320

Country of Origin: USA.
Type: Long-range jet transport.
Power Plant: Four 18,000 lb st (8 165 kgp) Pratt & Whitney JT3D-3 or 19,000 lb st (8 618 kgp) JT3D-7 turbofans.
Performance (-320C): Max cruising speed, 605 mph (973 km/h) at 25,000 ft (7 620 m); economical cruise, 550 mph (886 km/h); range with max passenger payload, 4,300 mls (6 920 km); range with max fuel and 147 passengers, 5,755 mls (9 265 km).
Accommodation: Flight crew of three or four and up to 219 passengers six-abreast with central aisle at a pitch of 29-in (74-cm).
Status: First 707-320 flown 11 January 1959, certificated 15 July 1959, entered service (Pan American) 26 August 1959. First 707-420 flown 20 May 1959, certificated (USA) 12 February and (UK) 27 April 1960; entered service (BOAC) May 1960. First 707B flown 31 January 1962, certificated 31 May 1962, entered service (Pan American) June 1962. First 707C flown 19 February 1963, certificated 30 April 1963, entered service (Pan American) June 1963. Production complete (except military variants).
Sales: Overall 707 sales total by 1983, 967, of which 86 military or non-commercial. Commercial 707-320 sales totalled 69 and 707-420, 37; 707-320B/-320C sales for commercial use totalled 482.
Notes: The Intercontinental 707-320 emerged as a longer version of the 707-120 with extra wing area, at first with turbojets but in its -320B and (with cargo door) -320C version, with turbofans. More than 400 Boeing 707s were in airline service in 1983, mostly -320Bs and -320Cs.

BOEING 707-320B

Dimensions: Span, 145 ft 8½ in (44,42 m); length, 152 ft 11 in (45.60 m); height, 42 ft 5½ in (12,94 m); wing area, 3,050 sq ft (283,4 m²).

Weights: Operating weight empty, 146,400 lb (66 406 kg); max payload, 53,900 lb (24 450 kg); max fuel, 159,260 lb (72 239 kg); max zero fuel, 230,000 lb (104 330 kg); max take-off, 33,600 lb (151 315 kg); max landing, 247,000 lb (112 037 km).

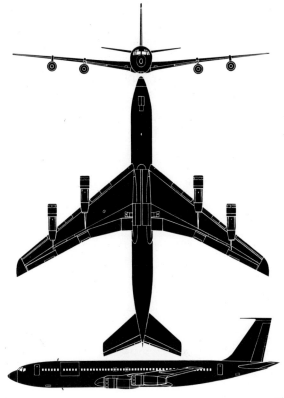

BOEING 727

Country of Origin: USA.

Type: Short/medium-range jet transport.

Power Plant: Three 14,500 lb st (6 577 kgp) Pratt & Whitney JT8D-9A or 15,500 lb st (7 031 kgp) JT8D-15 or 16,000 lb st (7 258 kgp) JT8D-17 or 17,400 lb st (7 893 kgp) JT8D-17R (with automatic thrust reserve) turbofans.

Performance (209,500-lb/95 030-kg take-off weight): Max cruise, 599 mph (964 km/h); economical cruise, 570 mph (917 km/h); range with max payload, 1,860 mls (2 993 km); range with max fuel, 2,510 mls (4 040 km).

Accommodation: Flight crew of three and up to 189 passengers six-abreast with central aisle, at 30-in (76-cm) seat pitch.

Status: First 727-100 flown on 9 February 1963, certificated on 24 December 1963 and entered service (Eastern Airlines) on 1 February and (United) 6 February 1964. First 727C (with cargo door and handling system) flown 30 December 1964, certificated 13 January 1966, entered service (Northwest Orient) 23 April 1966. First 727-200 flown 27 July 1967, certificated 29 November 1967, entered service (Northeast Airlines) 14 December 1967. First Advanced 727 flown 3 March 1972, certificated 14 June 1972, entered service (All Nippon Airways) July 1972. First flight with ATR, 27 May 1976. Production ends September 1984.

Sales: Grand total of 1,832 Boeing 727s sold includes 1,249 727-200 and Advanced 727-200s.

Notes: The Boeing 727 tri-jet, second of the Boeing family of jetliners, retains its lead as the world's best-selling civil transport, although sales are now declining as the Boeing 757 and 767 become available.

BOEING 727-200

Dimensions: Span, 108 ft 0 in (32,92 m); length, 153 ft 2 in (46,69 m); height, 34 ft 0 in (10,36 m), wing area, 1,700 sq ft (157,9 m²).

Weights: Operating weight empty (typical), 100,000 lb (45 360 kg); max payload, 40,000 lb (18 144 kg); standard fuel, 54,010 lb (24 498 kg); max fuel, 59,750 lb (27 102 kg); max zero fuel, 138,000–144,000 lb (62 595–65 315 kg); max take-off, 184,800–209,500 lb (83 820–95 027 kg); max landing, 154,500–161,000 lb (70 080–73 028 kg).

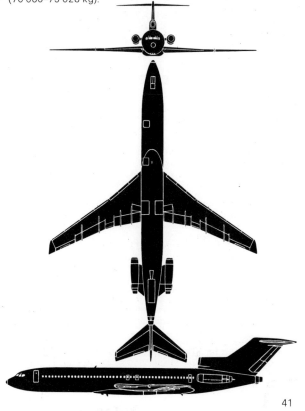

41

BOEING 737

Country of Origin: USA.

Type: Short/medium-range jet transport.

Power Plant: Two 14,500 lb st (6 577 kgp) Pratt & Whitney JT8D-9A or 15,500 lb st (7 031 kgp) JT8D-15 or 16,000 lb st (7 258 kgp) JT8D-17 or 17,400 lb st (7 893 kgp) JT8D-17R (with automatic thrust reserve) turbofans.

Performance (standard Advanced 737-200): Max cruise at mid-cruise weight, 576 mph (927 km/h) at 22,600 ft (6 890 m); economical cruise, 495 mph (796 km/h) at 30,000 ft (9 145 m); range with 115 passengers, 2,188 mls (3 521 km); range, high-gross weight version, 2,648 mls (4 262 km).

Accommodation: Flight crew of two or three at customer's option and up to 130 passengers six-abreast with central aisle at 29-in (74-cm) seat pitch.

Status: First 737-100 flown 9 April 1967 and first 737-200 (fifth 737) flown on 8 August 1967. Certification, -100 on 15 December 1967 and -200 on 21 December 1967. Entered service (-100, Lufthansa) on 10 February 1968 and (-200, United) 28 April 1968. First Advanced 737-200 flown on 15 April 1971, certificated 3 May and entered service (All Nippon Airways) June 1971.

Sales: Grand total of 1,027 Boeing 737s sold by early 1983, including 838 Model -200s and 89 Model 200Cs for commercial use. Production of 737-100 complete; 30 built.

Notes: Boeing 737 is the "baby" of the Boeing jetliner family, launched on 19 February 1965 on the basis of an order from Lufthansa, but the 737-100 specified by the German airline was quickly superseded by the 6-ft (1.82-m) longer 737-200. The "stretched" 737-300 is separately described.

BOEING 737-200

Dimensions: Span, 93 ft 0 in (28,35 m); length, 100 ft 2 in (30,53 m); height, 37 ft 0 in (11,28 m); wing area, 980 sq ft (91,04 m²).
Weights: Operating weight empty, 61,050 lb (27 691 kg); max payload, 33,300 lb (15 104 kg); max fuel, 39,855 lb (18 078 kg); max zero fuel, 95,000 lb (43 091 kg); max take-off, 115,500 lb–128,100 lb (52 390–58 105 kg); max landing, 103,000–107,000 lb (46 720–48 534 kg).

BOEING 737-300

Country of Origin: USA.

Type: Medium range jet transport.

Power Plant: Two 20,000 lb st (9 072 kgp) General Electric/SNECMA CFM56-C turbofans (flat-rated up to 86 deg F).

Performance: Cruising speeds, similar to Boeing 737-200 series; range with 140-passenger payload, 2,700 mls (4 353 km); range with max payload (high gross weight option), 1,900 mls (3 056 km).

Accommodation: Flight crew of two and up to 149 passengers six-abreast, with central aisle, at seat-pitch of 30-in (76-cm). Typical mixed class arrangement, eight first-class four-abreast at 38-in (96,5-cm) pitch and 120 tourist six-abreast at 32-in (81-cm) pitch.

Status: Full-scale development and production go-ahead 26 March 1981. First flight scheduled March 1984; certification and first deliveries November 1984.

Sales: Initial orders for 10 each (plus options) placed by US Air and Southwest Airlines in March 1981; five ordered by Orion Airways June 1982; three ordered by Western January 1983.

Notes: The 737-300 has been developed by Boeing to take advantage of the extra power offered by the CFM56 turbofans without an equivalent increase in fuel consumption. Thus it has been possible to offer a short/medium-range aircraft of increased passenger capacity but with greatly improved fuel efficiency. Wing chord is increased by four per cent, the shape and position of the engine nacelles has been modified and a number of smaller changes made to permit operation at higher gross weights. See previous entry for Boeing 737–200

BOEING 737-300

Dimensions: Span, 94 ft 10 in (28,91 m); length, 107 ft 7 in (33,40 m); height, 36 ft 6 in (11,13 m).
Weights: Operating weight empty, 70,675 lb (32 058 kg); max zero fuel, basic, 105,000 lb (47 625 kg); max zero fuel, option, 106,500 lb (48 308 kg); max take-off, basic, 124,500 lb (56 473 kg); max take-off, option, 130,000 lb (58 968 kg) or 135,000 lb (61 236 kg).

BOEING 747

Country of Origin: USA.

Type: Long-range large-capacity jet transport.

Power Plant (-200): Four 48,570 lb st (22 030 kgp) Pratt & Whitney JT9D-7AW or 50,000 lb (22 680 kgp) -7FW or -7J or 53,000 lb st (24 040 kgp) -7Q or 54,000 lb st (24 495 kgp) -7R4G2 or 52,500 lb st (23 815 kgp) General Electric CF6-50E, E1 or E2 or 50,100 lb st (22 725 kgp) Rolls-Royce RB.211-524B2 or 51,600 lb st (23 405 kgp) -524C2 or 53,100 lb st (24 085 kgp) -524D4 turbofans.

Performance: Max cruising speed, 584 mph (939 km/h) at 35,000 ft (10 670 m); economical cruise, 564 mph (907 km/h) at 35,000 ft (10 670 m); range with 452 passengers -200B at 805,000 lb (365 140-kg) take-off weight, 6,563 mls (10 562 km).

Accommodation: Flight crew of three and up to 550 passengers 11 abreast with two aisles at 34-in (86-cm) seat pitch.

Status: First 747 flown 9 February 1969, certificated 30 December 1969, entered service (Pan American) 21 January 1970. First -200 flown 11 October 1970, certificated 23 December 1970, entered service (KLM) early 1971. First 747F flown 30 November 1971, certificated 7 March 1972, entered service (Lufthansa) 7 March 1972. First 747C flown 23 March 1973, certificated 24 April 1973, entered service with World Airways. First 747SR flown 4 September 1973. First flight with CF6 engines 26 June 1973; first with RB.211 engines, 3 September 1976. First 747-300 (extended upper deck) flown 5 Oct 1982.

Sales: Total of 543 commercial sales by early 1983 comprising 165 -100, 35 -100B/SR, 207 -200B, 64 Combi, 18 -300, 11 -200C and 43 -200F. See next entry for 747SP.

BOEING 747-200B

Dimensions: Span, 195 ft 8 in (59,64 m); length, 225 ft 2 in (68,63 m); height, 63 ft 5 in (19,33 m); wing area, 5,500 sq ft (511 m²).

Weights: Operating weight empty, 391,000 lb (177 355 kg); max payload, 145,500 lb (66 000 kg); max fuel, 360,412 lb (163 480 kg); max zero fuel, 526,500 lb (238 815 kg); max take-off, 833,000 lb (377 840 kg); max landing, 630,000 lb (285 765 kg).

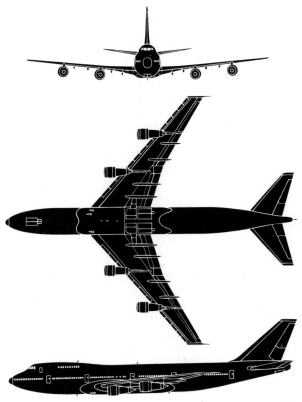

BOEING 747SP

Country of Origin: USA.

Type: Very long-range large-capacity transport.

Power Plant: Four 46,950 lb st (21 300 kgp) Pratt & Whitney JT9D-7A or 48,000 lb st (21 773 kgp) -7F or 58,750 lb st (22 113 kgp) -7AW or 50,000 lb st (22 680 kgp) -7FW or -7J, or 46,500 lb st (21 092 kgp) General Electric CF6-45A2/B2 or 50,100 lb st (22 725 kgp) Rolls-Royce RB.211-524B2 or 51,600 lb st (23 405 kgp) -524C2 or 53,110 lb st (24 090 kgp) -524D4 turbofans.

Performance: Max cruise, 581 mph (935 km/h) at 37,000 ft (11 280 m); economical cruise, 567 mph (913 km/h) at 37,000 ft (11 280 m); range with 331 passengers at 700,000 lb (317 515 kg) take-off weight, 6,736 mls (10 841 km); ferry range, 8,463 mls (13 620 km).

Accommodation: Flight crew of three and up to 440 passengers 11-abreast with two aisles at 30–34-in (76–86-cm) seat pitch; typical mixed class, 331, comprising 32 on upper deck, 28F and 271Y 10-abreast in main cabin.

Status: First 747SP flown on 4 July 1975, certificated 4 February 1976, entered service (Pan American) May 1976.

Sales: Total of 43 Boeing 747SPs sold to 11 airlines by the beginning of 1983.

Notes: The SP (for Special Performance) is the only variant of the Boeing 747 to differ dimensionally from the basic model (described in the previous entry). It was developed to meet airline requirements for a transport with a very long range but smaller capacity than the 747-200, having a fuselage shortened by 47 ft 1 in (14,35 m) but retaining 90 per cent commonality overall with the original aircraft.

BOEING 747SP

Dimensions: Span, 195 ft 8 in (59,64 m); length, 184 ft 9 in (56,31 m); ht, 65 ft 5 in (19,94 m); wg area, 5,500 sq ft (511 m²).
Weights: Typical operating weight empty, 326,000 lb (147 870 kg); max payload, 83,780 lb (38 000 kg); max fuel, 336,196 lb (152 496 kg); max zero fuel, 410,000–425,000 lb (185 973–192 777 kg); max take-off, 630,000–700,000 lb (285 765–317 515 kg); max landing, 450,000–465,000 lb (204 117–210 920 kg).

BOEING 757

Country of Origin: USA.

Type: Short/medium-range jet transport.

Power Plant: Two 37,400 lb st (16 965 kgp) Rolls-Royce RB.211-535C or RB.211-535E4 or 38,200 lb st (17 329 kgp) Pratt & Whitney PW 2037 turbofans.

Performance (RB.211 engines, basic aircraft): Max cruise, 569 mph (915 km/h) at 29,000 ft (8 839 m); long-range cruise, 528 mph (850 km/h) at 37,000 ft (11 278 m); max range with 178 passengers, 2,476 mls (3 984 km).

Accommodation: Flight crew of two and up to 233 passengers six-abreast with central aisle at 29-in (74-cm) seat pitch; typical mixed class layout for 178 with four-abreast at 38-in (97-cm) pitch and six-abreast at 34-in (86-cm) pitch.

Sales: First of five flight test and development aircraft flown on 19 February 1982 and second on 28 March 1982. Certification, (FAA) 21 December 1982, (CAA) 14 January 1983. First services (Eastern) 1 January 1983, (British Airways) 9 February 1983.

Sales: Total of 123 firm sales to seven airlines by 1983, comprising Air Florida, 3; British Airways, 19 (including two for Air Europe); Delta, 60; Eastern, 27; l ACSA, 2; Monarch, 3; Transbrasil, 9.

Notes: Boeing launched the 757 into full development and production on 23 March 1979. Earlier project activity had proceeded under the 7-N-7 generic title as Boeing searched for the correct formula for an aircraft designed to succeed the 727. The variant launched is the 757-200, with a choice of engines, and provision for later weight increases to 240,000 lb (108 860 kg) for greater payload-range when the uprated RB.211–535E4 and PW2037 engines became available.

BOEING 757-200

Dimensions: Span, 124 ft 6 in (37,95 m); length, 155 ft 3 in (47,32 m); height, 44 ft 6 in (13,56 m); wing area, 1,951 sq ft (181 m²).

Weights (RB-211 engines): Operating weight empty, 131,020 lb (59 430 kg); max payload, 64,000 lb (29 030 kg); max zero fuel, 184,000 lb (83 460 kg); max take-off, 220,000 lb (99 790 kg); max landing, 198,000 lb (89 810 kg).

BOEING 767

Country of Origin: USA.
Type: Medium-range jet transport.
Power Plant: Two 47,700 lb st (21 637 kgp) Pratt & Whitney JT9D-7R4D or 47,700 lb st (21 637 kgp) General Electric CF6-80A turbofans.
Performance (JT9D engines): Max cruise speed, 582 mph (937 km/h) at 30,000 ft (9 150 m); long-range cruise, 528 mph (850 km/h) at 39,000 ft (11 887 m); design range, basic -200, 3,201 mls (5 152 km), medium-range option, 2,297 mls (3 697 km), high gross weight option, 3,662 mls (5 893 km).
Accommodation: Flight crew of two and up to 255 passengers seven-abreast with two aisles at 30-in (76-cm) seat pitch; typical mixed-class layout for 18F, six-abreast at 38-in (96.5-cm) pitch, and 193Y seven-abreast at 34-in (86-cm) pitch.
Status: First 767-200 (company-owned, JT9D engines) flown 26 September 1982; three 767-200s (United Airlines, JT9D engines) for flight/test development flown 4 November, 28 December and 30 December 1982. Certification, 30 July 1982, entered service (United Airlines) 8 September 1981. First 767-200 with CF6 engines flown 19 February 1982, certificated 4 October.
Sales: Total of 177 Boeing 767-200s on order for 19 operators.
Notes: Launched into production on 14 July 1978 on the basis of an order by United Airlines (soon followed by American and Delta), the 767 resulted from several years of project development under the 7X7 designation. As well as the version launched, a 767-300 with longer fuselage had also been projected, but the 767-200 is the only variant ordered to date.

BOEING 767-200

Dimensions: Span, 156 ft 1 in (47,57 m); length, 159 ft 2 in (48,51 m); height, 52 ft 0 in (15,85 m); wing area, 3,050 sq ft (283,3 m²).

Weights (-200 basic): Operating weight empty, 180,300 lb (81 783 kg); max payload, 92,253 lb (41 845 kg); max zero fuel, 248,000 lb (112 490 kg); max take-off, 300,000 lb (136 080 kg); max landing, 270,000 lb (122 470 kg); max take-off, high gross weight options, 315,000–335,000 lb (142 884–151 956 kg).

BRITISH AEROSPACE ATP

Country of Origin: United Kingdom.
Type: Regional airliner.
Power Plant: Two 2,400 shp (1 790 kW) Pratt & Whitney PW124 turboprops.
Performance: Typical cruising speed, 295 mph (474 km/h); max range with capacity payload, 961 mls (1 547 km); typical unrefuelled mission, three 173-ml (278-km) stages with 64 passengers.
Accommodation: Flight crew of two and max high density arrangement for 72 passengers; typical layout, 64 passengers four-abreast at 31-in (79-cm) pitch, with central aisle.
Status: Prototype first flight third quarter of 1985. Entry into service March 1986.
Sales: No firm sales announced to end-1982. British Midland Airways has announced its "keen interest and support for development of the ... ATP", for which it has a prospective requirement for up to 12 as replacements for the Viscount and Fokker F27.
Notes: The ATP (Advanced Turboprop) airliner is a product of the Manchester Division of British Aerospace, being a derivative of the HS.748 (see previous entry). It has the same fuselage cross-section but is about 18 ft (5,49 m) longer to accomodate four more seat rows. The wing structure is the same, with revised wing-tips, and the vertical tail has slight sweepback. New engines have six-bladed propellers and an advanced technology flight deck is incorporated, designed to increase pilot efficiency and reduce workload through the use of push-button selector indication for system status with colour-coding, miniaturised engine instruments and automatic display of malfunctions.

BRITISH AEROSPACE ATP

Dimensions: Span, 100 ft 6 in (30,63 m); length, 85 ft 6 in (26,06 m); height, 24 ft 9 in (7,54 m).
Weights: Operating weight empty, 29,900 lb (13 563 kg); max payload, 13,600 lb (6 169 kg); max take-off, 48,700 lb (22 090 kg); max zero fuel, 43,500 lb (19 732 kg); max landing, 47,400 lb (21 501 kg).

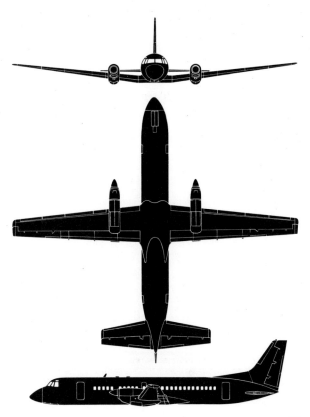

BRITISH AEROSPACE BAE 146

Country of Origin: United Kingdom.
Type: Short-range regional transport.
Power Plant: Four 6,700 lb st (3 040 kgp) Avco Lycoming ALF 502R-3 turbofans.
Performance (BAe 146-200): Max cruising speed, 482 mph (775 km/h) at 26,000 ft (7 925 m); long-range cruise, 436 mph (702 km/h) at 30,000 ft (9 145 m); range with max payload (typical reserves), 1,768 mls (2 845 km); range with max fuel (including options) 2,153 mls (3 465 km).
Accommodation: Flight crew of two; typical one-class seating for 82; max high density arrangement, 109 passengers.
Status: BAe 146-100 development aircraft flown 3 September 1981, 25 January 1982 and 2 April 1982; first BAe 146-200 flown 1 August 1982. Certification of -100 scheduled end-1982; certification of -200 early 1983.
Sales: Four -100 and 11 -200 on order plus 12 options. Early customers include Air Wisconsin and Dan-Air. Route proving by BAF completed January 1983. Certification 7 February 1983.
Notes: The BAe 146 was designed (as the HS.146) at Hatfield by Hawker Siddeley Aviation prior to latter's nationalization as part of British Aerospace, which launched production of the 146 in July 1978. Production is spread throughout BAe factories in the UK with final assembly at Hatfield; Avco Corp in USA and Saab-Scania in Sweden are producing wings and tail units respectively. Initial BAe 146-200 seats up to 93 and is some 8 ft (2,4-m) shorter; it is followed by the -200 which differs only in fuselage length and operating weights, and is expected to become the most numerous variant in service.

56

BAe 146-200

Dimensions: Span 85 ft 5 in (26,34 m); length, 93 ft 8½ in (28,56 m); height, 28 ft 3 in (8,61 m); wing area, 832 sq ft (77,30 m²).

Weights: Typical operating weight empty, 48,000 lb (21 773 kg); max payload, 24,000 lb (10 886 kg); max usable fuel, 15,000 lb (6 804 kg); max zero fuel, 69,250 lb (31 411 kg); max take-off, 88,250 lb (40 029 kg); max landing, 77,000 lb (34 927 kg).

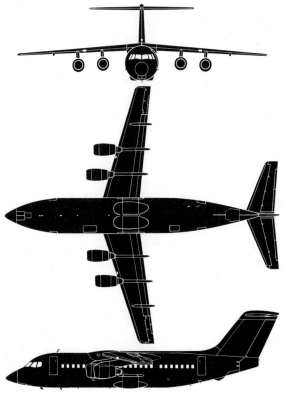

BRITISH AEROSPACE HS.748

Country of Origin: United Kingdom.
Type: Regional airliner.
Power Plant (Srs 2B): Two 2,280 ehp (1 982 kW) Rolls-Royce Dart RDa 7 Mk 536-2 turboprops.
Performance (Srs 2B): Max cruise, 290 mph (466 km/h) at 12,000 ft (3 660 m); long-range cruise, 269 mph (433 km/h) at 25,000 ft (7 620 m); max payload range, 1,324 mls (2 130 km) at cost economical cruise.
Accommodation: Normal flight crew of two and 48–52 passengers at 30-in (76-cm) pitch, four-abreast with central aisle.
Status: Two Avro 748 prototypes flown 24 June 1960 and 10 April 1961. First production Srs 1 flown 30 August 1961, certificated 7 December 1961, entered service with Skyways. Prototype Srs 2 flown 6 November 1961; certicated October 1962, entered service with BKS Air Transport. Prototype Srs 2C flown 31 December 1971. First production Srs 2B flown 22 June 1977.
Sales: Total of 18 Srs 1s built, Overall 748 sales total (military and civil), 360 by end of 1982 including those assembled by HAL in India.
Notes: The 748 has provided steady business for what was the Avro company, now Manchester Division of British Aerospace, since it entered production early in 1962. The Srs 1 had less powerful Dart engines and lower weights; Srs 2 and 2A differ in engine variants, Srs 2C has a large cargo loading door and Srs 2B has increased wing span and numerous product improvements. Introduced in 1983, the 748-2B Super has an advanced flight deck and engine hush-kits.

BRITISH AEROSPACE HS.748 SERIES 2B

Dimensions: Span, 102 ft 6 in (31,23 m); length, 67 ft 0 in (20,42 m); height, 24 ft 10 in (7,57 m); wing area, 828.87 sq ft (77,00 m²).

Weights: Typical operational empty, 26,814 lb (12 163 kg); max payload, 11,686 lb (5 300 kg); max zero fuel, 38,500 lb (17 464 kg); max take-off, 46,500 lb (21 092 kg); max landing, 43,000 lb (19 505 kg).

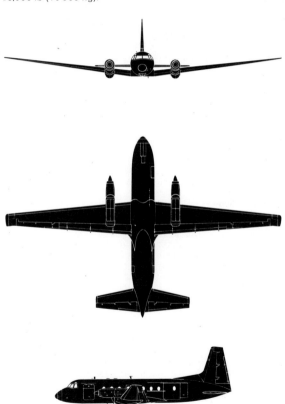

BRITISH AEROSPACE JETSTREAM 31

Country of Origin: United Kingdom.
Type: Commuter liner and business twin.
Power Plant: Two flat-rated 900 shp (671 kW) Garrett TPE 331-10 turboprops.
Performance: Max cruise, 300 mph (482 km/h) at 20,000 ft (6 100 m); long-range cruise, 265 mph (426 km/h) at 25,000 ft (7 620 m); max payload (18 passengers) range, 736 mls (1 185 km) at cost econ cruise.
Accommodation: Flight crew of two and up to 19 passengers three-abreast at 29-in (74-cm) pitch with offset aisle.
Status: Prototype (derived from original Handley Page production variant) first flown on 28 March 1980. First two production Jetstream 31s flown on 18 March and 26 May 1982 respectively. British certification, 29 June 1982. Production deliveries commenced December 1982 (to Contactair and Peregrine) and January 1983 ("green" aircraft to USA), with projected production rate building up to 25 a year during the course of 1984.
Sales: Seven plus 13 options and letters of intent. Initial customers for commuter version include Contactair (Germany), Partnair (Norway) and Peregrine Air Service (United Kingdom).
Notes: Jetstream 31 is the re-launched BAe production version of original HP.137, now being offered in 18/19-seat commuter, 12-seat executive shuttle and nine-seat corporate versions. Several examples of the earlier HP.137, some with US turboprops replacing the original Astazous, are still in airline use. Also projected is a version specially equipped to operate as an off-shore patrol aircraft to protect national EEZs (exclusive economic zones).

BRITISH AEROSPACE JETSTREAM 31

Dimensions: Span, 52 ft 0 in (15,85 m); length, 47 ft 2 in (14,37 m); height, 17 ft 6 in (5,37 m); wing area, 270 sq ft (25,08 m²).

Weights: Operational empty (commuter layout), 9,046 lb (4 103 kg); max payload, 4,182 lb (1 897 kg); max usable fuel, 3,079 lb (1 397 kg); max zero fuel, 13,228 lb (6 000 kg); max take-off and landing, 14,550 lb (6 600 kg).

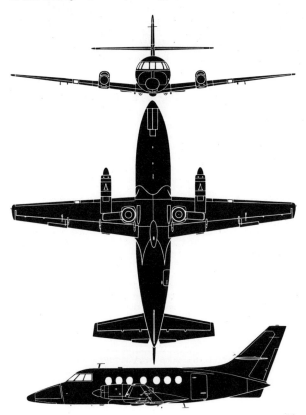

BRITISH AEROSPACE (BAC) ONE-ELEVEN

Country of Origin: United Kingdom.
Type: Short-range jet transport.
Power Plant (Srs 500): Two 12,550 lb st (5692 kgp) Rolls-Royce Spey 512 DW turbofans.
Performance (Srs 500): Max cruise, 541 mph (870 km/h) at 21,000 ft (6400 km); best economy cruise, 472 mph (760 km/h) at 35,000 ft (10670 m); range with typical max payload, 1,694 mls (2726 km); max range, 2,212 mls (3560 km).
Accommodation: Flight crew of two and up to 119 passengers five-abreast, with off-set aisle, at 29-in (74-cm) pitch.
Status: Prototype first flown 20 August 1963; first production Srs 200 flown 19 December 1963, certification 6 April 1965 followed by first services on 9 April (BUA) and 25 April (Braniff). Prototype Srs 300/400 flown 13 July 1965; Srs 400 certification 22 November 1965. Prototype Srs 500 flown 30 June 1967 and first production Srs 500 on 7 February 1968 and certificated 18 August 1968. Prototype Srs 475 flown 27 August 1970 and first production on 5 April 1971, with certification in July. Production in UK complete. First Srs 560 flown in Romania 18 September 1982.
Sales: Total of 230 built in UK including 56 Srs 200, nine Srs 300, 69 Srs 400, nine Srs 475 and 87 Srs 500.
Notes: One-Eleven Srs 200, 300 and 400 are dimensionally similar; Srs 500 has longer fuselage and extended wing tips and Srs 475 has original fuselage with extended wing and uprated engines. Following delivery of last One-Eleven in mid-1982, British Aerospace is supplying components for 22 more to be assembled in Romania.

BRITISH AEROSPACE (BAC) ONE-ELEVEN -500

Dimensions: Span, 93 ft 6 in (28,50 m); length, 107 ft 0 in (32,61 m); height, 24 ft 6 in (7,47 m); wing area, 1,031 sq ft (95,78 m²).

Weights: Typical operating empty, 53,762 lb (24 386 kg); max payload, 27,238 lb (12 355 kg); max zero fuel, 81,000 lb (36 741 kg); max take-off, 104,500 lb (47 400 kg); max landing, 87,000 lb (39 463 kg).

CANADAIR CL-44

Country of Origin: Canada.

Type: Long-range cargo and passenger transport.

Power Plant: Four 5,730 shp (4 272 kW) Rolls-Royce Tyne 515/10 turboprops.

Performance: Cruising speed, 386 mph (621 km/h) at 20,000 ft (6 100 m); range with max payload, 3,260 mls (5 245 km); range with max fuel and 35,564-lb (16 132-kg) payload, 5,587 mls (8 990 km).

Accommodation: Flight crew of three and up to 189 passengers six-abreast with central aisle at 32-in (81-cm) pitch.

Status: First CL-44D (military CC-106) flown 15 November 1959; first CL-44D-4 (commercial prototype) flown 16 November 1960; first delivery (Flying Tiger) 31 May 1961. CL-44J prototype flown 8 November 1965, CL-44-O conversion flown 26 November 1969. Production completed.

Sales: Total of 27 CL-44D-4s built for Flying Tiger, Seaboard World, Slick and Loftleider.

Notes: Original CL-44D was a Canadian development from the Bristol Britannia design, with lengthened fuselage, greater wing span and new engines. Twelve were built for the RCAF as CC-106 Yukons, several passing into commercial service as freighters when retired in 1973. The CL-44D-4 was built primarily as a commercial freighter, featuring a swing-tail for straight-in loading. Loftleider used CL-44s as high density transports, including four CL-44J conversions with stretched fuselage for 214 passengers. The sole CL-44-O has an enlarged diameter upper deck. About a dozen CL-44Ds and Yukons were still in airline service, as freighters, in 1983.

CANADAIR CL-44D-4

Dimensions: Span, 142 ft 3½ in (43,37 m); length, 136 ft 10¾ in (41,73 m); height, 38 ft 8 in (11,80 m); wing area, 2,075 sq ft (192,72 m²).

Weights: Operating weight empty, 88,952 lb (40 345 kg); max payload, 63,272 lb (28 725 kg); max fuel, 81,448 lb (36 944 kg); max zero fuel, 155,000 lb (70 308 kg); max take-off, 210,000 lb (95 250 kg); max landing, 165,000 lb (74 843 kg).

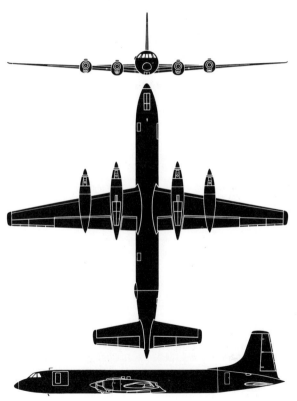

CASA C-212 AVIOCAR

Country of Origin: Spain.
Type: Commuter airliner and general purpose light transport.
Power Plant: Two 900 shp (671 kW) Garrett TPE 331-10-501-C turboprops.
Performance: Max cruise, 220 mph (354 km/h) at 10,000 ft (3 050 m); long range cruise, 193 mph (311 km/h) at 10,000 ft (3 050 m); max payload range (26 passengers), 230 mls (370 km).
Accommodation: Flight crew of two and 22 passengers at 28.5-in (72-cm) pitch three abreast with offset aisle or 26 passengers at 28.5-in (72-cm) pitch four abreast with central aisle.
Status: Prototype C-212 flown 26 March 1971; 138th and 139th production aircraft became prototypes for the Srs 200, the first of these flying on 30 April 1978. Deliveries of Srs 200 commenced early 1980. Production at beginning of July 1982 was running at five monthly (including kits for licence assembly by PT Nurtanio of Indonesia).
Sales: By the beginning of September 1982, a total of 325 C-212s had been ordered (all versions), of which approximately half to civil customers in 16 different countries; 240 of this total had been delivered, including about 60 for commuter airline use in the USA.
Notes: Possessing STOL characteristics, the C-212 is available in several civil and military versions. The original Srs 100 had lower-rated TPE 331-5 engines and a gross weight of 12,500 lb (5 675 kg) or, eventually, 14,330 lb (6 500 kg). In Indonesia, PT Nurtanio assembled 29 Srs 100 aircraft before part-manufacture (up to 85 per cent of the total airframe) and final assembly switched to the Srs 200.

CASA C-212 AVIOCAR

Dimensions: Span, 62 ft 4 in (19,00 m); length, 49 ft 10½ in (15,20 m); height, 20 ft 8¾ in (6,32 m); wing area, 430.56 sq ft (40,00 m²).

Weights: Operational empty, 10,053 lb (4560 kg); max zero fuel, 15,542 lb (7050 kg); max take-off, 16,424 lb (7450 kg); max landing, 16,203 lb (7350 kg).

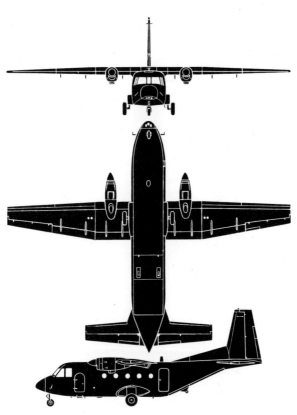

CASA-NURTANIO CN-235

Country of Origin: Spain and Indonesia.
Type: Regional airliner and general purpose transport.
Power Plant: Two flat-rated 1,700 shp (1 268 kW) General Electric CT7-7 turboprops.
Performance: Max cruise, 282 mph (454 km/h) at 20,000 ft (6 100 m); range at max cruise power at 20,000 ft (6 100 m), 921 mls (1 482 km) with 34 passengers and 690 mls (1 112 km) with 38 passengers.
Accommodation: Flight crew of two and up to 38 passengers at 30-in (76-cm) pitch or 34 passengers at 32-in (81-cm) pitch, four-abreast with central aisle.
Status: Two prototypes under construction, scheduled for simultaneous first flights in Spain and Indonesia in October 1983. Certification and first flight of initial production aircraft scheduled for second quarter of 1984, with deliveries commencing November 1984.
Sales: Fifty-four orders (plus 18 options) announced by end-1982. Customers include Merpati Nusantara (14); Pelita (10); Deraya Air Taxi (10); and Iberia/Aviaco/Transeurope (20). The Indonesian government has ordered 32 for military duties.
Notes: Development of the CN-235 was launched as a jointly-funded programme by CASA in Spain and PT Nurtanio in Indonesia, as a larger follow-up for the C-212 Aviocar, which is built in both countries. Designed to meet military as well as civil needs, it features a rear-loading ramp, and a stretched derivative to carry up to 59 passengers is also planned for later introduction. Production is shared, without duplication, by CASA and PT Nurtanio, with final assembly lines in each country.

CASA-NURTANIO CN-235

Dimensions: Span, 84 ft 7½ in (25,80 m); length, 69 ft 10¼ in (21,30 m); height, 25 ft 10¾ in (7,90 m).
Weights: Max (cargo) payload, 9,920 lb (4500 kg); max fuel, 8,818 lb (4000 kg); max zero fuel weight, 26,014 lb (11800 kg); max take-off, 28,658 lb (13000 kg); max landing, 28,218 lb (12800 kg).

CESSNA 404 TITAN

Country of Origin: USA.
Type: Light commuter and cargo transport.
Power Plant: Two 375 hp (280 kW) Continental GTSIO-520-M flat-six piston engines.
Performance: Max cruise, 229 mph (369 km/h) at 10,000 ft (3 050 m); economical cruising speed, 161 mph (259 km/h) at 10,000 ft (3050 m) and 188 mph (302 km/h) at 20,000 ft (6 100 m); range with max fuel, up to 2,115 mls (3 404 km).
Accommodation: Up to eight individual seats and one two-passenger bench seat, including one or two pilots' seats.
Status: Prototype first flown 26 February 1975. Deliveries began October 1976.
Sales: About 350 sold by early 1983, for business and commercial use.
Notes: The Titan is one of several Cessna business twins that have applications as commuterliners and for air taxi work. The standard passenger-carrying version is known as the Titan Ambassador; The Titan Courier is a utility passenger/cargo version and the Titan Freighter has a specially hardened interior for cargo-carrying. Among the other Cessna twins that have found favour with airline and air taxi operators are the Model 310 series of five-six seaters; the eight/ten-seat Model 402 and the pressurized nine-seat Models 414A Chancellor and 421C Golden Eagle. More recently, two turpoprop twins have joined the range, these being the pressurized Model 425 Conquest I (originally named Corsair) with PT6A-112 engines and the Model 441 Conquest II (which is the original Conquest) with 636 shp (474 kW) TPE 331-8-401S engines.

CESSNA 404 TITAN

Dimensions: Span, 46 ft 4 in (14,12 m); length, 39 ft 6¼ in (12,04 m); height, 13 ft 3 in (4,04 m); wing area, 242 sq ft (22,48 m).

Weights: Empty weight (Ambassador), 4,834 lb (2 192 kg), (Courier), 4,861 lb (2 205 kg), (Freighter), 4,702 lb (2 133 kg); max fuel, 2,270 lb (1 030 kg); max zero fuel, 8,100 lb (3 674 kg); max take-off, 8,400 lb (3 810 kg); max landing, 8,100 lb (3 674 kg).

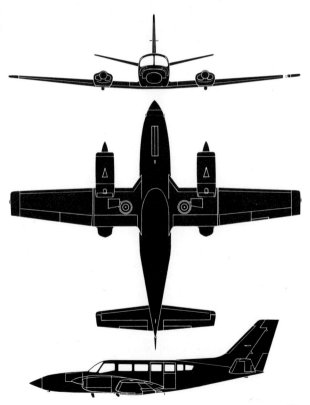

CONVAIR CV-440 METROPOLITAN

Country of Origin: USA.

Type: Short-range piston-engined airliner.

Power Plant: Two 2,500 hp (1 867 kW) Pratt & Whitney R-2800-CB17 air cooled piston engines.

Performance: Max cruise, 300 mph (483 km/h) at 13,000 ft (3 962 m); economical cruise, 280 mph (451 km/h) at 16,000 ft (4 877 m); range with max (44-passenger) payload, 120 mls (193 km); range with max fuel, 1,520 mls (2 446 km).

Accommodation: Flight crew of two or three, and up to 56 passengers four-abreast with central aisle at 30-in (76-cm) or 32-in (81-cm) pitch.

Status: Prototype (Model 110) flown 8 July 1946; first production (Model 240) flown 16 March 1947; first service (American Airlines) 1 June 1948. First CV-340 flown 5 October 1951, entered service 28 March 1952. Prototype CV-440 flown 6 October 1955, first production CV-440 flown 15 December 1955, entered service (Continental Airlines) February 1956. Production completed.

Sales: Total production, 176 CV-240 (plus 39 non-commercial); 212 CV-340 (plus 99 non-airline); CV-440, 153 (plus 26 non-commercial).

Notes: The Convair 240 was developed to the specific requirements of American Airlines as a post-war successor to the DC-3 and enjoyed modest success in the three related versions noted above, the CV-340 and CV-440 being a little larger in overall dimensions. About 50 remain in service, principally CV-440s, on the American continent. The later turboprop-conversions with Allison 501 or Rolls-Royce Dart engines are described separately on the next page.

CONVAIR CV-440

Dimensions: Span, 105 ft 4 in (31,12 m); length, 81 ft 6 in (24,84 m); height, 28 ft 2 in (8,59 m); wing area, 920 sq ft (85,5 m²).

Weights: Basic operating, 33,314 lb (15 110 kg); max payload, 12,836 lb (5 820 kg); max fuel, 10,380 lb (4 708 kg); max zero fuel, 47,000 lb (21 319 kg); max take-off, 49,700 lb (22 544 kg); max landing, 47,650 lb (21 614 kg).

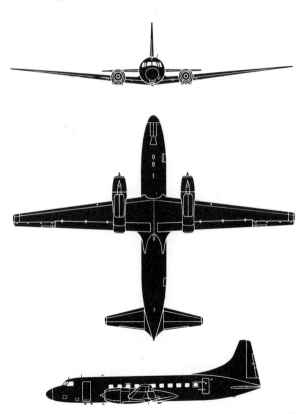

CONVAIR 580 (AND 600, 640)

Country of Origin: USA.
Type: Short-range turboprop airliner.
Power Plant: Two, 3,750 shp (2 800 kW) Allison 501-D13H turboprops.
Performance: Max cruise, 342 mph (550 km/h) at 20,000 ft (6 100 m), range with 5,000-lb (2 270-kg) payload, 2,866 mls (4 611 km).
Accommodation: Flight crew of two or three, and up to 56 passengers four-abreast with central aisle, at 30-in (76-cm) pitch.
Status: CV-240 Turboliner prototype flown 29 December 1950 and YC-131C conversion with Allison 501D turboprops flown 29 June 1954; first CV-580 Allison-Convair flown 19 January 1960, certificated 21 April 1960 and entered airline service (Frontier) June 1964. Eland-Convair conversion flown 9 February 1955, entered airline service (Allegheny) July 1959. CV-600 (Dart engines) first flown 20 May 1965, certificated 18 November, entered service (Central Airlines) 30 November 1965; CV-640 first flown 20 August 1965, certificated 7 December 1965, entered service (Caribair) 22 December 1965.
Sales: Total of 170 CV-340s/440s converted to CV-580 of which 110 for airline use. Total of 38 CV-240s converted to CV-600 and 27 CV-340s/440s to CV-640s, for airline use.
Notes: Several schemes for converting piston-engined airliners to have turboprop engines were projected during the 'fifties, but only the Convair 240/340/440 family was adopted for such conversion on a large scale. Nearly 100 CV-580s were still in airline service in 1983, together with about 40 of the Dart-engined CV-600s and CV-640s.

CONVAIR 580

Dimensions: Span, 105 ft 4 in (32,12 m); length, 81 ft 6 in (24,84 m); height, 29 ft 2 in (8,89 m); wing area, 920 sq ft (85,5 m²).

Weights: Operating weight empty, 30,275 lb (13 732 kg); max payload, 8,870 lb (4 023 kg); max fuel, 13,887 lb (6 299 kg); max take-off, 58,140 lb (26 371 kg); max landing, 52,000 lb (23 187 kg).

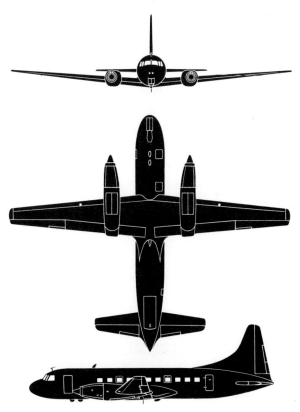

COMMUTER AIRCRAFT CORP CAC-100

Country of Origin: USA.

Type: Regional airliner.

Power Plant: Four Pratt & Whitney PT6A-65R turboprops, each flat-rated at 1,200 shp (896 kW).

Performance: Max cruising speed, 353 mph (569 km/h) at 15,000 ft (4 570 m); range (with 50 passengers), 638 mls (1 028 km).

Accommodation: Flight crew of two and 50 passengers at 32-in (84-cm) pitch four-abreast with central aisle. High density capacity, 60 passengers.

Status: Construction of manufacturing facility has begun at Youngstown, where CAC will assemble one or more prototypes from major assemblies built under sub-contract. First flight expected early in 1984 and entry into service mid-1985.

Sales: None announced up to end-1982.

Notes: The CAC-100 has its origins in a slightly smaller but similar design originally promoted as the GAC-100 by General Aircraft Corp under Dr Lynn Bollinger, who had developed the range of Helio STOL lightplanes. In CAC, the project has been master-minded by Kornel Feher, now company president, and final design definition and refinement was handled by Ladislao Pazmany as chief engineer. Latest features are shown in the general arrange-ment drawing and include lengthening of the fuselage, extension of the inboard nacelles, rearrangement of the doors and use of uprated engines. A full production launch depended upon the company obtaining adequate financing, pending which construc-tion of an assembly and manufacturing plant was put in hand at Youngstown, Ohio.

COMMUTER AIRCRAFT CORPORATION CAC-100

Dimensions: Span, 74 ft 10 in (22,81 m); length, 72 ft 1 in (21,97 m); height, 25 ft 8½ in (7,65 m); wing area, 501.5 sq ft (46,59 m²).

Weights: Typical operating empty, 22,815 lb (10 350 kg); max (structural limit) payload, 12,150 lb (5 511 kg); max take-off, 37,500 lb (17 010 kg).

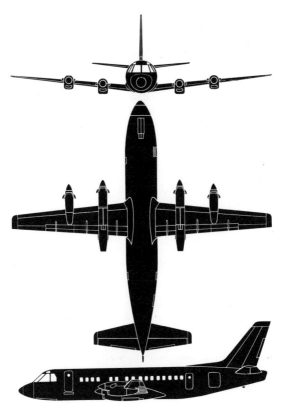

CURTISS C-46

Country of Origin: USA.
Type: Piston-engined freighter and utility transport.
Power Plant: Two 2,000 hp Pratt & Whitney R-2800-34 air-cooled radial engines.
Performance: Max speed, 269 mph (433 km/h); typical cruising speed, 187 mph (301 km/h) at 7,000 ft (2 133 m) at mean weight of 45,000 lb (20 412 kg); range with max payload, 110 mls (177 km); range with max fuel and 5,700-lb (2 585-kg) payload, 1,170 mls (1 883 km).
Accommodation: Flight crew of two; original layouts provided for 40 passengers four-abreast at 41-in (104-cm) pitch with central aisle or up to 62 five-abreast at 35-in (89-cm) pitch with offset aisle.
Status: Prototype CW-20 first flown 26 March 1940; first military C-46 flown late summer 1941. Production ended 1945.
Sales: Total of 3,141 C-46 Commandoes built for USAF, of which many hundreds acquired post-war for airline use. Approximately 60-70 in use 1982.
Notes: The portly C-46 originated as a Curtiss private venture in 1938, with a single prototype built in airliner configuration. Production was exclusively to military requirements during World War II, although the CW-20 prototype went into airline service in 1942 with BOAC. Built as military troop and supply transports, the C-46s proved especially attractive post-war as capacious low-cost freighters, and small numbers remain in service in this rôle in 1983, mostly in Latin America, despite ageing airframes and spares shortages that make servicing and maintenance increasingly difficult.

CURTISS C-46

Dimensions: Span, 108 ft 0 in (32,92 m); length, 76 ft 4 in (23,27 m); height, 21 ft 8 in (6,60 m); wing area, 1,358 sq ft (126 m²).

Weights: Typical empty equipped, 33,000 lb (14 970 kg); max payload, 11,630 lb (5 265 kg); max fuel, 8,400 lb (3 810 kg); max zero fuel, 45,148 lb (20 488 kg); max take-off (freighter) 48,000 lb (21 772 kg); max landing, 46,800 lb (21 228 kg).

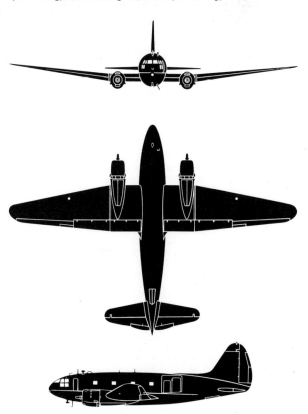

DASSAULT-BREGUET MERCURE

Country of Origin: France.
Type: Short-range jet transport.
Power Plant: Two 15,500 lb st (7030 kgp) Pratt & Whitney JT8D-15 turbofans.
Performance: Max cruise, 579 mph (932 km/h) at 20,000 ft (6 100 m); best economy cruise, 533 mph (858 km/h) at 30,000 ft (9 145 m); range with max payload, 1,230 mls (1 980 km); range with max fuel, 2,300 mls (3 700 km).
Accommodation: Flight crew of two; typical mixed-class seating, 12F four-abreast at 38-in (96,5-cm) pitch and 108 Y six-abreast at 32-in (81,5-cm) pitch; maximum passenger capacity 162 at 30-in (76-cm) pitch.
Status: Two prototypes flown 28 May 1971 and 7 September 1972. First production aircraft flown 17 July 1973, certificated 12 February 1974, entered service (Air Inter) 4 June 1974. Certificated for Cat III operation 30 September 1974. Production completed.
Sales: Ten aircraft ordered by Air Inter 29 January 1972, all still in service 1982; no other sales.
Notes: The Mercure was intended by Dassault to provide a basis for the company to expand its commercial activities and was put into production with only one airline order, placed by the French domestic operator Air Inter. Consequently, considerable losses were made on the programme by Dassault and the French government, as well as risk-sharing partners in Italy, Spain, Belgium, Switzerland and Canada. An attempt to launch a developed Mercure 200 with McDonnell Douglas participation did not succeed.

DASSAULT-BREGUET MERCURE

Dimensions: Span, 100 ft 3 in (30,55 m); length, 114 ft 3$\frac{1}{2}$ in (34,84 m); height 37 ft 3$\frac{1}{4}$ in (11,36 m); wing area, 1,249 sq ft (116,0 m²).

Weights: Operating empty, 70,107 lb (31 800 kg); max payload, 35,715 lb (16 200 kg); max zero fuel, 105,820 lb (48 000 kg); max take-off, 124,560 lb (56 500 kg); max landing, 114,640 lb (52 000 kg).

DE HAVILLAND CANADA TWIN OTTER

Country of Origin: Canada.
Type: Commuter and light transport.
Power Plant: Two 652 shp (487 kW) Pratt & Whitney PT6A-27 turboprops.
Performance: Max cruise, 209 mph (337 km/h) at 10,000 ft (3 050 m); long-range cruise, 170 mph (274 km/h) at 10,000 ft (3 050 m); range with max payload, 161 mls (259 km).
Accommodation: Flight crew of one or two and up to 20 passengers seated at 30-in (76-cm) pitch three-abreast.
Status: Prototype first flown 20 May 1965; certification May 1966, initial deliveries July 1966. production rate 4–5 a month during 1982.
Sales: Total, more than 800 by end-1982, including military and non-airline commercial sales. First 115 aircraft were Series 100, next 115 were Series 200, thereafter Series 300.
Notes: As its name suggests, the DHC-6 Twin Otter began life as a twin-engined derivative of the single piston-engined Otter, with which it shares some wing and fuselage components. It has proved to have excellent appeal in the commuter and third-level airline market, with its STOL performance allowing it to bring reliable scheduled service to many close-in town airports. Original Series 100 had shorter nose and Series 300 introduced the uprated PT6A-27 engines. Floatplane, skiplane and amphibious versions are avilable, and de Havilland has developed a Srs 300M Twin Otter for more specifically military rôles, with wing strong points and provision for a search radar under the nose. This version, and some Srs 300s in civilian but non-airline use, operate at a higher gross weight.

DE HAVILLAND CANADA TWIN OTTER

Dimensions: Span, 65 ft 0 in (19,81 m); length, 51 ft 9 in (15,77 m); height, 18 ft 7 in (5,66 m); wing area, 420 sq ft (39,02 m²).

Weights: Operational empty, 7,415 lb (3 363 kg); max payload, 4,520 lb (2 050 kg); max zero fuel, 12,300 lb (5 579 kg); max take-off, 12,500 lb (5 670 kg); max landing, 12,300 lb (5 579 kg).

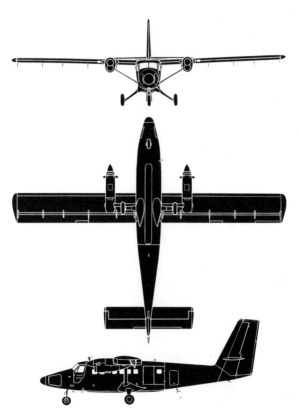

DE HAVILLAND CANADA DASH 7

Country of Origin: Canada.
Type: STOL regional airliner.
Power Plant: Four 1,120 shp (835 kW) Pratt & Whitney PT6A-50 turboprops.
Performance: Max cruise, 265 mph (427 km/h) at 10,000 ft (3 050 m); long-range cruise, 250 mph (399 km/h) at 20,000 ft (6 100m); range (with 50-passenger payload), 840 naut mls (1 352 km).
Accommodation: Flight crew of two and up to 56 passengers at 29-in (74-cm) pitch four-abreast with central aisle.
Status: Two prototypes first flown 27 March and 26 June 1975 respectively. First production aircraft flown 30 May 1977, entered service 3 February 1978 (with Rocky Mountain Airways). Production rate between two and three a month.
Sales: Total of more than 130 sold.
Notes: The Dash-7 (DHC-7) is among the largest of the regional airliners at present in service, matching the British Aerospace HS.748 and Fokker F27 in capacity but offering STOL performance, which it derives from the use of double slotted flaps operating in the slipstreams from four large-diameter, slow-running five-bladed propellers. Basic aircraft is the Series 100; a few Series 101s are in all-cargo configuration and DHC-7R Ranger is specially equipped for the Canadian Coast Guard. Projected Series 200 has more powerful (1,500 shp) PT6As and higher gross weight, while the Series 300 under study by the end of 1982 for possible introduction in 1986 would have a fuselage stretched by 18 ft 6 in (5,6 m) to seat up to 78 passengers, and a gross weight of 52,700 lb (23 900 kg).

DE HAVILLAND CANADA DASH 7

Dimensions: Span, 93 ft 0 in (28,35 m); length, 80 ft 8 in (24,58 m); height, 26 ft 3 in (8,00 m); wing area, 860 sq ft (79,9 m²).

Weights: Operational empty, 27,690 lb (12 560 kg); max payload 11,306 lb (5 127 kg); max zero fuel, 39,000 lb (17 690 kg); max-take-off, 44,000 lb (19 958 kg); max landing, 42,000 lb (19 051 kg).

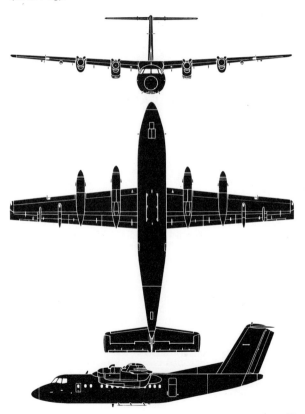

DE HAVILLAND CANADA DASH 8

Country of Origin: Canada.
Type: STOL regional airliner.
Power Plant: Two flat-rated 1,788 shp (1,333 kW) Pratt & Whitney PW120 turboprops.
Performance: Max cruise, 311 mph (500 km/h) at 15,000 ft (4 570 m); range with max payload (36 passengers), 447 mls (720 km) at 5,000 ft (1 525 m) with three intermediate landings and no refuelling; max range, 1,266 mls (2 038 km).
Accommodation: Flight crew of two and up to 36 passengers at 31-in (79-cm) pitch four-abreast with central aisle.
Status: Prototypes under construction, for planned first flight June 1983. First customer delivery mid-1984. Production planning to permit a rate of six a month to be reached by early 1986.
Sales: Orders for 45 aircraft plus 79 options by January 1983. First customer NorOntair, the air service of the Ontario Northland Transport Commission.
Notes: The Dash 8 (DHC-8) is the latest in the Canadian company's successful series of small transports with special STOL capabilities. It has been designed to serve as a junior partner with the Dash 7, with which it shares a similar configuration, featuring a high wing and T-tail. Like the larger aircraft, the Dash 8 depends upon large-area trailing edge flaps and a sophisticated control system for its low-speed performance and control, without use of leading-edge flaps. Intended primarily for use by the regional airlines, the Dash 8 is also being offered in executive versions, and with mixed passenger/cargo layouts including quick-change options. The entire accommodation area is pressurized and provision is made for single-pilot operation.

DE HAVILLAND CANADA DASH 8

Dimensions: Span, 84 ft 0 in (25,60 m); length, 73 ft 0 in (22,25 m); height, 25 ft 0 in (7,62 m); wing area, 585 sq ft (54,30 m²).
Weights: Operational empty. 20,176 lb (9152 kg); max payload, 7,824 lb (3549 kg); max usable fuel, 5,750 lb (2608 kg); max zero fuel, 28,000 lb (12701 kg); max take-off, 30,500 lb (13835 kg); max landing, 30,000 lb (13608 kg).

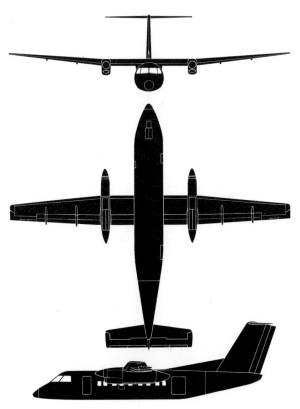

DORNIER DO 228

Country of Origin: Federal Germany.
Type: Commuter airliner.
Power Plant: Two flat-rated 715 shp (533 kW) Garrett TPE 331-5 turboprops.
Performance: (Do 228–200) Max cruise, 230 mph (370 km/h) at sea level, 268 mph (432 km/h) at 10,000 ft (3 050 m); long-range cruise, 206 mph (332 km/h) at 10,000 ft (3 050 m); max payload range (19 passengers), 715 mls (1 150 km).
Accommodation: Flight crew of two and (−100) 15 or (−200) 19 passengers at 30-in (76-cm) pitch, two-abreast with central aisle.
Status: The prototypes of the Do 228-100 and -200 flew respectively on 18 March and 9 May 1981, with deliveries of the former (to A/S Norving), commencing summer 1982. Production rate of five aircraft monthly (-100 and -200 combined) scheduled to be attained in 1983.
Sales: Firm orders and options for the two versions of the Do 228 totalled some 90 by late 1982, all in commuter airliner version, and including about 30 on firm order. Sales about equally divided between Scries 100 and Series 200.
Notes: Mating a new-technology wing of supercritical section with the fuselage cross section of the utility Do 128 and a retractable nosewheel undercarriage, the Do 228 is being manufactured in two versions, the -100 and -200, these differing only dimensionally in length. This unpressurised regional airliner and utility aircraft has large-span single-slotted Fowler flaps and flaperons. Military versions, including one equipped for maritime surveillance, are also available.

88

DORNIER DO 228

Dimensions: Span, 55 ft 7 in (16,97 m); length (-100), 49 ft 3 in (15,03 m), (-200), 54 ft 3 in (16,55 m); height, 15 ft 9 in (4,86 m); wing area, 344.46 sq ft (32,00 m²).
Weights: Operational empty, 7,370 lb (3 343 kg); max payload, 4,870 lb (2 207 kg); max zero fuel, 11,900 lb (5 400 kg); max take-off, 12,570 lb (5 700 kg); max landing, 12,570 lb (5 700 kg).

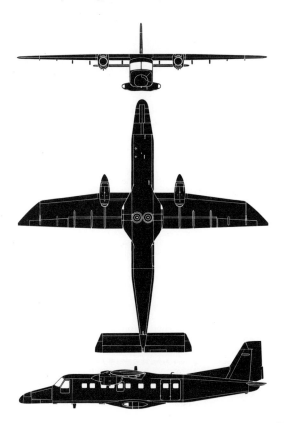

DOUGLAS DC-3

Country of Origin: USA.
Type: Short-range passenger and freight transport.
Power Plant: Two 1,200 shp Pratt & Whitney R-1830-92 Twin Wasp air-cooled radial engines.
Performance (Typical commercial operation, post-war): Max speed, 215 mph (346 km/h); economical cruise, 165 mph (266 km/h) at 6,000 ft (1 830 m); range with max payload, 300 mls (483 km); range with max fuel, 1,100 mls (1 770 km).
Accommodation: Flight crew of two; typical passenger layout provides for 28–32, four-abreast at up to 38-in (96,5-cm) pitch with central aisle.
Status: DST (prototype for DC-3 series) first flown 17 December 1935; first service use (American Airlines) 25 June 1936. Production completed 1946.
Sales: Total of 10,655 built, including 430 for commercial customers prior to December 1941, 10,197 for military use before and during World War II and 28 assembled post-war from surplus components as DC-3Ds. About 400 were still in airline service at the end of 1982.
Notes: The DC-3 established an outstanding reputation in the five years before the USA entered World War II, as the most efficient and comfortable short-medium range airliner then available. Adopted for military use, it gained more fame as the C-47 Skytrain and the Dakota, and many thousands were civilianized after the war ended to provide the backbone of the air transport industry in the early post war years. They have proved almost indestructible, and still in 1983 play a part in the air transport system of many nations, especially in the Third World.

DOUGLAS DC-3

Dimensions: Span, 95 ft 0 in (28,96 m); length, 64 ft 6 in (19,66 m); height, 16 ft 11½ in (5,16 m); wing area, 987 sq ft (91,7 m²).

Weights: Typical operating weight empty, 19,300 lb (8 755 kg); max payload, 6,600 lb (2 994 kg); max fuel, 4,820 lb (2 186 kg); max take-off, 28,000 lb (12 700 kg); max landing, 26,900 lb (12 202 kg).

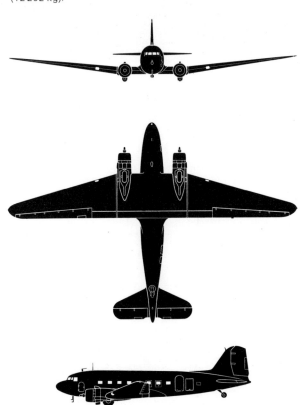

DOUGLAS DC-4

Country of Origin: USA.
Type: Medium-range passenger and freight transport.
Power Plant: Four 1,450 hp (1 082 kW) Pratt & Whitney R-2000-2SD-13G air-cooled radial engines.
Performance: Max speed, 265 mph (426 km/h); max cruising speed, 204 mph (328 km/h) at 10,000 ft (3 050 m) at mean weight of 65,000 lb (29 484 kg); range with max payload, 1,150 mls (1 850 km); range with max fuel and 5,480-lb (2 486-kg) payload, 2,180 mls (3 510 km).
Accommodation: Flight crew of two or three; 66–86 passengers five-abreast with offset aisle.
Status: DC-4E prototype first flown 21 June 1938. Revised DC-4 first flown (as military C-54) 14 February 1942. First commercial service (American Overseas Airlines) October 1945. Production completed August 1947.
Sales: Total of 1,165 military variants built (C-54, C-114, C-116), plus 79 DC-4-1009s post-war for commercial use (and 71 C-54Ms by Canadair). Many hundred C-54s civilianized post-war, with a few dozen still in airline service in 1982.
Notes: The DC-4 was designed to meet requirements of US domestic airlines for a larger, longer-range transport to complement the DC-3, but its development was overtaken by World War II and commercial operations did not begin until 1945. The DC-4 was widely used in the 'forties and 'fifties by airlines throughout the world and a few still remain in service where low cost is more important than modern standards of comfort and speed. The DC-4 was also the basis for development of the Canadair C-54M with Merlin engines and the ATL Carvair vehicle transport.

DOUGLAS DC-4

Dimensions: Span, 117 ft 6 in (35,82 m); length, 93 ft 5 in (28,47 m); height, 27 ft 7 in (8,41 m); wing area, 1,462 sq ft (135,8 m²).

Weights: Typical empty equipped, 46,000 lb (20 865 kg); max payload, 14,200 lb (6 440 kg); max fuel, 21,520 lb (9 761 kg); max zero fuel, 63,500 lb (28 800 kg); max take-off, 73,000 lb (33 112 kg); max landing, 63,500 lb (28 800 kg).

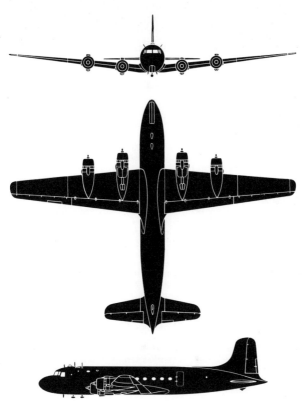

DOUGLAS DC-6 (AND DC-7)

Country of Origin: USA.

Type: Medium to long-range passenger and freight transport.

Power Plant: Four 2,400 hp (1 790 kW) Pratt & Whitney R-2800-CA-15 air-cooled radial engines.

Performance: Max cruising speed, 316 mph (509 km/h); typical economical cruise, 280 mph (451 km/h) at 16,000 ft (4 877 m) at mean weight of 83,000 lb (37 650 kg); range with max payload, 2,150 mls (3 450 km); max range, 2,770 mls (4 458 km).

Accommodation: Flight crew of three or four; typically 68–86 passengers five-abreast with offset aisle.

Status: Prototype (military XC-112) first flown 15 February 1946; first production DC-6 flown June 1946, first airline service (United) 17 April 1947. DC-6A first flown 29 September 1949, entered service (Slick) 16 April 1951; DC-6B first flown 2 February 1951, entered service (American) 29 April 1951. DC-7 first flown 18 May 1953, entered service (American) 29 November 1953; DC-7B first flown 25 April 1955, entered service (Pan American) 23 May 1955; DC-7C first flown 20 December 1955, entered service (Pan American) 1 June 1956. Production completed (DC-6) February 1959 (DC-7) December 1958.

Sales: Total of 1,042 DC-6/7 variants built, including 174 DC-6, 73 DC-6A, 288 DC-6B, 168 Military, 106 DC-7, 112 DC-7B and 121 DC-7C.

Notes: DC-6 and DC-7, in their successive sub-variants, were progressive extrapolations of the DC-4, with same configuration but various fuselage lengths. Nearly 100 DC-6s were still in commercial service at the end of 1982, but only a handful of DC-7s were then surviving.

DOUGLAS DC-6B

Dimensions: Span 117 ft 6 in (35,81 m); length, 105 ft 7 in (32,2 m); height, 29 ft 3 in (8,92 m); wing area, 1,463 sq ft (135,9 m²).

Weights: Basic operating weight, 58,635 lb (26 595 kg); max payload, 24,565 lb (11 143 kg); max fuel, 32,950 lb (14 946 kg); max zero fuel, 83,200 lb (37 740 kg); max take-off, 107 000 lb (48 534 kg); max landing, 88,200 lb (40 007 kg).

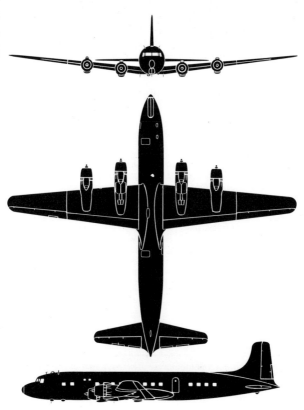

EMBRAER EMB-110 BANDEIRANTE

Country of Origin: Brazil.
Type: Regional airliner.
Power Plant: Two flat-rated 750 shp (560 kW) Pratt & Whitney PT6A-34 turboprops.
Performance: Max cruise, 244 mph (393 km/h) at 8,000 ft (2 438 m); long-range cruise 216 mph (348 km/h) at 10,000 ft (3 050 m); may payload (19 passengers) range, (P1) 230 mls (370 km), (P2) 267 mls (430 km).
Accommodation: Flight crew of two and (P1 and P2) 19 passengers three-abreast at 31-in (79-cm) pitch.
Status: Military prototypes first flown 26 October 1968, 19 October 1969 and 26 June 1970; first production EMB-110 flown 9 August 1972; first airline use (15-seat EMB-110C) 16 April 1973. Stretched EMB-110P2 first flown 3 May 1977. Production rate, approx six a month.
Sales: Total EMB-110 deliveries (military and civil) exceed 400, including nearly 200 P1 and P2 commuters to 60 operators world wide.
Notes: The unpressurized Bandeirante originated to a Brazilian military specification as the first substantial aircraft design and production programme undertaken wholly in Brazil. It was available at the right moment to meet expanding commuterliner markets, in which it has sold well. EMB-110P2 is basic all-passenger (up to 21) version, P1 has larger rear loading door for passenger/cargo convetible operations. Original certification basis for the commercial Bandeirante was FAR-23 at 12,500 lb (5 670 kg) gross weight; the recertificated EMB-110/41 (to SFAR 41) operates at weights quoted here.

EMBRAER EMB-110 BANDEIRANTE

Dimensions: Span, 50 ft 3 in (15,32 m); length, 49 ft 6½ in (15,10 m); height 16 ft 1¾ in (4,92 m); wing area, 313.25 sq ft (29,10 m²).

Weights: Operational empty (P1), 8,010 lb (3 630 kg), (P2) 7,915 lb (3 590 kg); max payload (P1), 3,600 lb (1 633 kg), (P2), 3,443 lb (1 561 kg); max zero fuel, 12,015 kg (5 450 kg); max take-off, 13,010 lb (5 900 kg); max landing, 12,566 lb (5 700 kg).

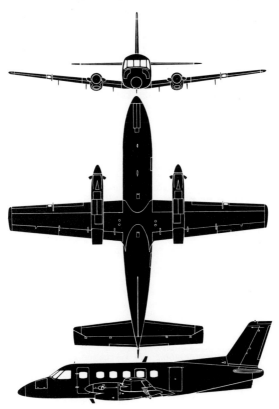

EMBRAER EMB-120 BRASILIA

Country of Origin: Brazil.
Type: Regional airliner.
Power Plant: Two 1,500 shp (1120 kW) Pratt & Whitney Canada PW115 turboprops.
Performance: Max cruise, 337 mph (537 km/h) at 20,000 ft (6 095 m); long-range cruise, 300 mph (482 km/h) at 20,000 ft (6 095 m); max payload range (30 passengers), 628 mls (1 010 km) at econ cruise; max fuel range, 1,820 mls (2 926 km) with 3,080-lb (1 400-kg) payload.
Accommodation: Flight crew of two and 30 passengers at 31-in (79-cm) pitch three-abreast with offset aisle. Optional arrangements for 24 and 26 passengers with enlarged baggage compartment.
Status: First prototype Brasilia scheduled to enter flight test on 29 July 1983; certification expected in the second half of 1984 and first customer deliveries from early 1985.
Sales: More than 100 orders and options claimed by early 1983, from 23 operators in eight countries (Brazil, USA, Finland, France, Australia, Colombia, Mexico and UK).
Notes: Design work on the EMB-120 Brasilia was launched in September 1979, the structural design having been finalised in January 1982. An all-cargo version is on offer and proposed versions include a corporate transport and military models for maritime surveillance, aeromedical evacuation, electronic intelligence, paratroop transportation and search and rescue. Flight testing of the PW115 engine, fitted in a representative Brasilia nacelle mounted on the nose of a Viscount, began in Canada on 27 February 1982.

EMBRAER EMB-120 BRASILIA

Dimensions: Span, 64 ft 10¾ in (19,78 m); length 65 ft 7⅖ in (20,00 m); height, 20 ft 10 in (6,35 m); wing area, 409.46 sq ft (38,03 m²).

Weights: Operational empty, 12,300 lb (5 580 kg); max payload, 6,000 lb (2 722 kg); max zero fuel, 8,600 lb (18 959 kg); max take-off and landing, 21,164 lb (9 600 kg).

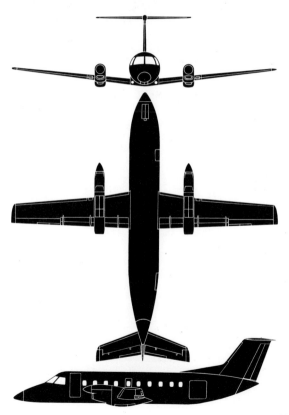

FAIRCHILD F-27 AND FH-227

Country of Origin: USA.

Type: Short-range turboprop transport.

Power Plant (FH-227): Two 2,230 eshp (1 664 kW) Rolls-Royce Dart 532-7 or (FH-227D, E) 2,300 eshp (1 716 kW) Dart 532-7L turboprops.

Performance (FH-227E): Max crusing speed, 294 mph (473 km/h) at 15,000 ft (4 570 m); best economy cruise, 270 mph (435 km/h) at 25,000 ft (7 620 m); range with max payload, 656 mls (1 055 km); range with max fuel, 1,655 mls (2 660 km).

Accommodation: Flight crew of two (optionally, three) and up to 52 passengers four-abreast with central aisle at 31-in (79-cm) pitch, or a maximum of 56.

Status: Prototype Fairchild-built F27s flown 12 April and 23 May 1958; FAA certification 16 July 1958, entered service (West Coast Airlines) 27 September 1958. First FH-227 flown 27 January 1966; entered service (Mohawk) mid-1966. Production completed December 1968.

Sales: Fairchild built 128 F27s, plus a complete rebuild of first prototype after accidental damage, and 78 FH-227s.

Notes: Fairchild acquired a licence to build the Fokker F27 (see separate entry) on 26 April 1956 and put the aircraft into production at the same time as the parent company, actually achieving first deliveries and airline service before Fokker's own Friendships. Variants up to F-27M were built or projected, all with the same basic dimensions and varying Dart models. Fairchild also was first to develop a stretched variant, as the FH-227, nearly two years before Fokker flew the first Mk 500, with slightly less "stretch".

FAIRCHILD FH-227

Dimensions: Span, 95 ft 2 in (29,00 m); length, 83 ft 8 in (25,50 m); height, 27 ft 7 in (8,41 m); wing area, 754 sq ft (70,0 m²).

Weights: Operating weight empty, 22,923 lb (10 398 kg); max payload, 11,200 lb (5 080 kg); max fuel, 8,920 lb (4 046 kg); max zero fuel, 41,000 lb (18 600 kg); max take-off, 45,500 lb (20 639 kg); max landing, 45,000 lb (20 412 kg).

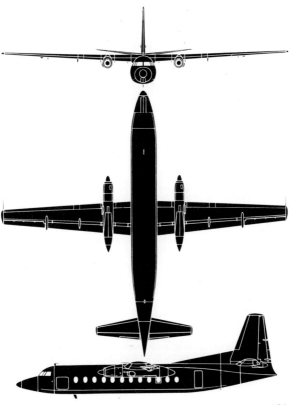

FAIRCHILD METRO III

Country of Origin: USA.
Type: Commuter airliner.
Power Plant: Two (Metro III) 1,000 shp (746 kW) Garrett TPE-331-11U-601G turboprops, or (Metro IIIA) 1,100 shp (820 kW) Pratt & Whitney PT6A-45R turboprops.
Performance: (Metro III) Max cruise, 317 mph (511 km/h) at 15,000 ft (4 575 m); long-range cruise, 286 mph (460 km/h) at 18,000 ft (5 485 m); max payload range (19 passengers), 1,000 mls (1 612 km) at cost econ cruise.
Accommodation: Flight crew of two and 19 passengers at 30-in (76-cm) pitch two-abreast with central aisle.
Status: Metro prototype first flown 26 August 1969; certification 11 June 1970. Customer deliveries began 1973 (Air Wisconsin). Metro II introduced 1974; Metro IIA certificated to SFAR-41 23 June 1980. Metro III entered service 1981. Metro IIIA first flown 31 December 1981. Metro production rate averaged four monthly during 1982.
Sales: Total of 239 Metros of all versions delivered, including 43 Metro IIIs up to mid-1982.
Notes: Metro III differs from earlier Metros in having a new, longer-span wing and more efficient engines, and Metro IIIA marks first use of Pratt & Whitney engines in this family of commuter aircraft. Both are certificated to SFAR-41B at weights shown above. Earlier Metro I and Metro II were limited to 12,500 lb (5670 kg) gross weight by FAR Part 23 regulations. The name Merlin is used for variants of the basic Metro design furnished for corporate/business use, and a variant specially equipped to operate in the maritime surveillance rôle is named the Air Sentry.

FAIRCHILD METRO III

Dimensions: Span, 57 ft 0 in (17,37 m); length, 59 ft 4¼ in (18,09 m); height, 16 ft 8 in (5,08 m); wing area, 309 sq ft (28,71 m²).

Weights: Operational empty (III) 8,737 lb (3 963 kg), (IIIA), 8,823 lb (4 022 kg); max payload (III), 3,763 lb (1 707 kg); max zero fuel (III & IIIA), 12,500 lb (5 670 kg); max take-off (III & IIIA), 14,500 lb (6 577 kg); max landing (III & IIIA), 14,000 lb (6 350 kg).

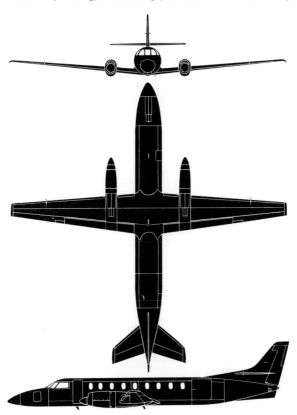

FOKKER F27 FRIENDSHIP

Country of Origin: Netherlands.
Type: Short-range turboprop transport.
Power Plant: (Mk 500/600): Two 2,320 shp (1 730 kW) Rolls-Royce Dart 536-7R turboprops.
Performance: Max cruise at 38,000-lb (17 237-kg) weight (Mk 500/600), 298 mph (480 km/h) at 20,000 ft (6 100 m); long-range cruise, 267 mph (430 km/h) at 20,000 ft (6 100 m); range with max payload (Mk 500), 520 mls (840 km); range with 44 passengers (Mk 600), 1,175 mls (1 890 km).
Accommodation: Flight crew of two (optionally, three) and up to 59 (Mk 600) or 60 (Mk 500) passengers four-abreast with central aisle at 29-in (74-cm) pitch.
Status: Two F27 prototypes first flown 24 November 1955 and 29 January 1957 respectively; US certification, 29 October 1957. First production F27 flown 23 March 1958; entered service (Mk 100 with Aer Lingus) 15 December 1958. Mk 200 first flown 20 September 1959; Mk 500 first flown 15 November 1967; Mk 600 first flown 28 November 1968. In production 1983.
Sales: Total of 534 F27s built by Fokker (and 205 by Fairchild) to 1983, including about 200 military/government agency and corporate. Totals include 85 Mk 100, 113 Mk 200, 13 Mk 300, 217 Mk 400/600, 95 Mk 500 and 11 Maritime.
Notes: Fokker F27 is the best-selling turboprop airliner (excluding Soviet types possibly built in larger numbers). Original Mk 100 was complemented by more powerful Mk 200, and the current Mk 600 is similar but has a cargo-loading door. Mk 400 is primarily military. Mk 500 has longer fuselage and also features the cargo door like the Mk 600.

FOKKER F27 FRIENDSHIP Mk 600

Dimensions: Span, 95 ft 2 in (29,00 m); length, 77 ft 3½ in (23,56 m); height, 27 ft 10¾ in (8,50 m); wing area, 754 sq ft (70,0 m²).

Weights: Operating empty, 26,781 lb (12 148 kg); max payload, 12,719 lb (5 769 kg); standard fuel, 9,090 lb (4 125 kg); max internal fuel, 13,180 lb (5 980 kg); max zero fuel, 39,500 lb (17,917 kg); max take-off, 45,000 lb (20 412 kg); max landing, 41,000 lb (18 598 kg).

FOKKER F28 FELLOWSHIP

Country of Origin: Netherlands.
Type: Regional jet airliner.
Power Plant: Two 9,900 lb st (4 490 kgp) Rolls-Royce RB.183-2 Mk 555-15P turbofans.
Performance: (Mk 4000 at 63,934 lb/29 000 kg gross weight): Max cruising speed, 524 mph (843 km/h) at 23,000 ft (7 000 m); econ cruising speed, 421 mph (678 km/h) at 30,000 ft (9 150 m); range with max payload (85 passengers), long-range cruise, 1,296 naut mls (2 085 km).
Accommodation: Flight crew of two; max one-class seating for 85 passengers, five-abreast, at 29-in (74-cm) pitch.
Status: Prototypes first flown on 9 May and 3 August 1967 respectively; pre-production standard F28 flown 20 October 1967. Certification and first delivery (to LTU) 24 February 1969. First Mk 4000 high-density long-fuselage variant flown 20 October 1976.
Sales: Total of 190 F28s sold in all variants (including military) up to end of 1982.
Notes: F28 was developed and put into production as Fokker's first jet transport, to complement the highly successful F27 turboprop twin. The Mk 4000, for which data are given here, is of particular interest to regional airlines, and has been sold to such operators in the USA, the Far East, Africa and Europe. The Mk 2000, no longer in production, has the same fuselage length, Mk 1000 and Mk 3000 have a length of 43 ft 0 in (13,10 m) and up to 65 passengers. During 1982, Fokker was studying possible stretched versions of the F28 for future development, with improved RB.183-03 Tay engines.

FOKKER F28 FELLOWSHIP

Dimensions: Span, 82 ft 3 in (25,07 m); length, 97 ft 1¾ in (29,61 m); height, 27 ft 9½ in (8,47 m); wing area, 850 sq ft (79,00 m²).

Weights: Operating empty, 38,683 lb (17 546 kg); max payload, 23,317 lb (10 576 kg); standard fuel, 17,240 lb (7 820 kg); max fuel, 23,080 lb (10 469 kg); max zero fuel, 62,000 lb (28 122 kg); max take-off, 73,000 lb (33 110 kg); max landing, 69,500 lb (31 524 kg).

GAF NOMAD 22 AND 24

Country of Origin: Australia.
Type: Commuter airliner and general utility light transport.
Power Plant: Two flat-rated 400 shp (298 kW) Allison 250-B17B turboprops.
Performance: (N24A) Max cruise, 193 mph (311 km/h) at 10,000 ft (3 050 m); long-range cruise, 169 mph (272 km/h) at 10,000 ft (3 050 m); max payload range (16 passengers), 639 mls (1 029 km) at cost econ cruise of 184 mph (297 km/h).
Accommodation: Flight crew of two and up to (N22B) 12 or (N24A) 16 passengers in single seats arranged each side of central aisle.
Status: Two N22 prototypes flown 23 July and 5 December 1971 respectively. First production N22 flown 3 October 1974 and certified May 1975 (with FAA certification on 20 May 1977). First stretched N24 flown 17 December 1975. Production rate between one and two a month in 1982/83, secheduled to terminate end-1984 at total of 170.
Sales: Firm sales total, 150 in April 1982, including all versions; about half of these for commercial use, principally small airlines in Australia and Pacific territories, plus a few N24 Commuterliners in the USA.
Notes: The Nomad is notable for its STOL performance and has sold in several military versions as well as for airline and specialised commercial use. N22B and N24A differ principally in length, as indicated above. One N22B has been flown with amphibious floats. Production will end in 1984 under a government decision announced mid-1982 to allow GAF to concentrate on military programmes.

GAF NOMAD 22 AND 24

Dimensions: Span, 54 ft 0 in (26,46 m); length (N22B), 41 ft 2½ in (12,50 m), (N24A), 47 ft 1 in (14,35m); height 18 ft 1½ in (5,52 m); wing area, 324 sq ft (30,10 m²).

Weights: (N24A) Operational empty, 5,436 lb (2 466 kg); max payload, 3,600 lb (1 633 kg); max usable fuel, 1,793 lb (813 kg); max zero fuel, 9,150 lb (4 151 kg); max take-off, 9,400 lb (4 265 kg); max landing, 9,200 lb (4 174 kg).

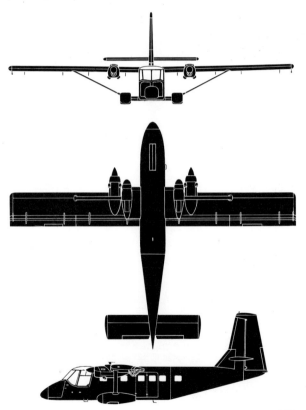

GRUMMAN G-111

Country of Origin: USA.

Type: Light transport amphibian.

Power Plant: Two 1,475 hp (1 100 kW) Wright R-1820-982C9HE3 air-cooled piston radial engines.

Performance: Economical cruise, 186 mph (300 km/h) at 5,000 ft (1 525 m); range with max (28-passenger) payload, 314 mls (506 km) from water take-off.

Accommodation: Flight crew of two and up to 28 passengers, basically arranged in seats four-abreast with centre aisle at 32-in (81-cm) pitch.

Status: Prototype (military XJR2F-1) first flown 24 October 1947. First G-111 conversion flown 13 February 1979, certificated 29 April 1980, entered service (Chalk's International Airlines) July 1981.

Sales: More than 50 available for conversion: initial sales to Resort International (Chalks) and Pelita Air Services.

Notes: The G-111 amphibian is a civilianized HU-16 Albatross, the latter being a search-and-rescue and general utility aircraft built in large quantities for the USAF and US Navy. Grumman developed the conversion package for surplus HU-16s initially in co-operation with Resorts International which required such aircraft for use by its subsidiary Chalk's on scheduled services between Florida and Nassau. Up to 200 aircraft are available for conversion, of which Grumman had acquired 57 by end-1982 and had delivered five. A turboprop version, with 1,645 shp Garrett TPE 331-15 engines, has been projected and would have improved performance as well as a 2,000-lb (907-kg) increase in useful load. A prototype was expected to fly before the end of 1983.

GRUMMAN G-111

Dimensions: Span, 96 ft 8 in (29,46 m); length, 61 ft 3 in (18,67 m); height, 25 ft 10 in (7,87 m); wing area, 1,035 sq ft (96,15 m).

Weights: Empty equipped, 23,500 lb (10 660 kg); may payload (cargo), over 8,000 lb (3 630 kg); max fuel, 6,438 lb (2 920 kg); max take-off, 30,800 lb (13 970 kg) from land, 31,150 lb (14 129 kg) from water; max landing, 29,160 lb (13 226 kg) on land, 31,150 lb (14,129 kg) on water.

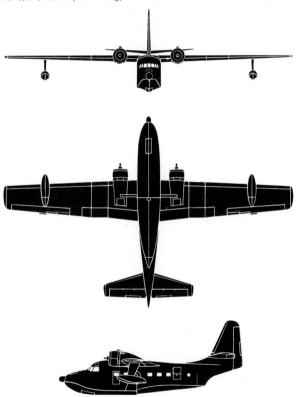

GRUMMAN MALLARD

Country of Origin: USA.

Type: Short-range amphibious transport.

Power Plant: Two 600 hp Pratt & Whitney R-1340-53H1 piston radial engines.

Performance: Max speed, 215 mph (346 km/h) at 6,000 ft (1 830 m); cruising speed, 180 mph (290 km/h) at 8,000 ft (2 438 m); range with max fuel, 1,380 mls (2 220 m).

Accommodation: Flight crew of two and up to eight passengers in individual seats in cabin.

Status: First G-73 Mallard flown 1946. Production complete.

Sales: Total of 61 built. About 10–12 in airline service in 1983, principally with Chalks International Airline.

Notes: The Mallard is an early post-war product of the Grumman company, which was attempting to perpetuate its pre-war line of small transport amphibians. Most of those built were purchased for private or business use but the surviving examples now include nine operated by Chalks International Airline on its scheduled services between Florida and the Bahamas. Three of the nine are Turbo Mallards, having been converted (by Frakes Aviation) to have PT6A-34 engines in place of the original piston engines, and Chalks planned eventually to have the entire fleet so converted. Previously, Chalks had been one of the larger operators of pre-war Goose amphibians. A few dozen of these 8-passenger aircraft, some converted by McKinnon Enterprises to have Pratt & Whitney PT6A turboprop engines (see silhouette) are still used by small airlines and air taxi operators, mostly in North America and Alaska. Also still to be found in service, mostly in Canada and Alaska, are a few of the smaller Widgeon amphibians.

GRUMMAN G-73 MALLARD

Dimensions: Span, 66 ft 8 in (20,32 m); length, 48 ft 4 in (14,73 m); height, 18 ft 9 in (5,72 m); wing area, 444 sq ft (41,25 m²).
Weights: Operating weight empty, 9,350 lb (4 245 km); max fuel, 2,537 lb (1 151 kg); max take-off, 12,750 lb (5 789 kg); max landing, 12,750 lb (5 789 kg).

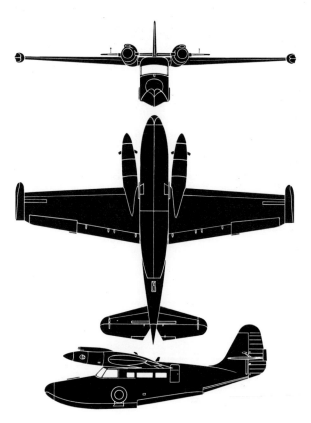

GULFSTREAM AEROSPACE G1-C

Country of Origin: USA.
Type: Commuter airliner and general purpose transport.
Power Plant: Two 1,900 eshp (1,417 kW) Rolls-Royce Dart Mk 529 turboprops.
Performance: Max cruise, 344 mph (554 km/h) at 25,000 ft (7 620 m); long-range cruise, 290 mph (467 km/h) at 25,000 ft (7 620 m); max payload range (37 passengers), 690 mls (1 112 km).
Accommodation: Flight crew of two and 37 passengers at 30-in (76-cm) pitch, three-abreast with offset aisle.
Status: Prototype G1-C (converted from standard Gulfstream I airframe) flown on 25 October 1979; first series conversion delivered (to Air North) on 11 November 1980, after certification on 30 October.
Sales: Two conversions (from some 190 Gulfstream I corporate transports still flying) each sold to Air North, Air US and Chaparral Airlines.
Notes: The G1-C is a stretched conversion of the Gulfstream I, production of which ended in 1968 with 200 built; first flown on 14 August 1958, the Gulfstream I was intended solely as a corporate transport, although a few saw some airline service (see photograph). In 1982, Orion Air was using 10 of these original aircraft as freighters for its small-package delivery service. Plans to produce new production G-1Cs on existing Gulfstream I tooling have been achieved by Gulfstream Aerospace, which acquired the rights from Grumman. Optional mixed passenger/freight and all-freight versions of the G1-C with large rear side cargo door have been offered.

GULFSTREAM AEROSPACE G1-C

Dimensions: Span, 78 ft 4 in (23,87 m); length, 75 ft 4 in (22,97 m); height, 22 ft 11 in (6,98 m); wing area, 610 sq ft (56,67 m²).

Weights: Operational empty, 24,850 lb (11 272 kg); max payload, 7,400 lb (3 357 km); max fuel, 10,415 lb (4 724 kg); max zero fuel, 32,250 lb (14 629 kg); max take-off, 36,000 lb (16 330 kg); max landing, 34,285 lb (15 552 kg).

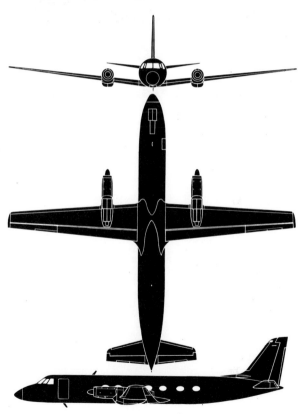

HANDLEY PAGE HERALD

Country of Origin: United Kingdom.

Type: Short-range turboprop transport.

Power Plant: Two 2,150shp (1 603 kW) Rolls-Royce Dart 527 turboprops.

Performance: Max cruise, 274 mph (441 km/h) at 15,000 ft (4 572 m); best economy cruise, 265 mph (426 km/h) at 23,000 ft (7 010 m); range with max payload, 280 mls (450 km); range with max fuel, 870 mls (1 400 km).

Accommodation: Flight crew of two and up to 56 passengers, four-abreast with central aisle at 34-in (86-cm) pitch.

Status: Piston-engined Herald prototypes flown on 25 August 1955 and 3 August 1956; prototypes with Dart engines flown 11 March and 17 December 1958. First production Srs 100 flown 30 October 1959, entered service (Jersey Airlines) 17 May 1961. Prototype lengthened Srs 200 flown 8 April 1961; first production Srs 200 flown 13 December 1961, entered service (Jersey Airlines) January 1962. Production completed August 1968.

Sales: Total of 50 built including two prototypes, four Srs 100 and eight Srs 400 (military), plus 36 Srs 200.

Notes: The Herald was one of several small transports developed in the late 'fifties as DC-3 replacements, but suffered a false start with four Alvis Leonides Major piston engines, in which form the two prototypes were first flown. With two Dart turboprops instead, it competed directly with the Avro 748 and Fokker F27, but had sold less well than either up to the time the Handley Page company ceased trading. By 1982, principal Herald operators were Air UK and BAF, the latter having leased several to other companies.

HANDLEY PAGE HERALD 200

Dimensions: Span, 94 ft 9 in (28,88 m); length, 75 ft 6 in (23,01 m); height, 24 ft 1 in (7,34 m); wing area, 886 sq ft (82,3 m²).

Weights: Operating weight empty, 25,800 lb (11 700 kg); max payload, 11,242 lb (5 100 kg); max zero fuel, 37,500 lb (17 010 kg); max take-off, 43,000 lb (19 505 kg); max landing, 39,500 lb (17 917 kg).

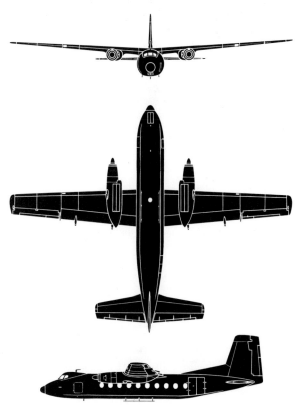

HARBIN Y-11T

Country of Origin: China.

Type: Light utility transport.

Power Plant: Two 620 shp Pratt & Whitney PT6A-27 turboprops.

Performance (Y-11T2): Max speed, 188 mph (302 km/h); cruising altitude, 9,842 ft (3 000 m); range with 17 passengers and baggage, 255 mls (410 km).

Accommodation: Two pilots on flight deck and up to 17 passengers three-abreast at a pitch of 31.5 in (80 cm), with offset aisle.

Status: First Y-11T1 prototype (PT6A-11 engines) flown in 1981 and second prototype on 14 July 1982. Certification to FAR Pts 23 and 135 under way in 1983.

Sales: No details announced. Production planned to meet Chinese domestic requirements.

Notes: The Y-11T has been developed at the Harbin (Binjiang) works of the State Aircraft Factories from the Y-11, which appeared in 1977 and is powered by Housai 6-A piston radial engines. The Y-11T differs in having a lengthened fuselage with curved sides, and turboprop engines. The first prototypes, known as Y-11T1s, have 500 shp PT6A-11 engines (derated to 475 shp), the production aircraft with more powerful PT6A-27s are designated Y-11T2s. The original Y-11 has been produced in limited numbers, for general duties including crop-dusting and spraying, in which rôles the Y-11T2 can also be used. The latter is also to be offered in the international market through the China National Aero Technology Import and Export Corporation and will be distributed in Europe by DK China New Products, a company associated with DK Aviation.

HARBIN Y-11T2

Dimensions: Span, 56 ft 6½ in (17,23 m); length, 48 ft 9 in (14,86 m); height, 17 ft 3½ in (5,28 m); wing area, 369 sq ft (34,27 m²).

Weights: Operating weight empty, 6,614 lb (3 000 kg); max fuel, 2,646 lb (1 200 kg); max payload, 3,748 lb (1 700 kg); max take-off weight, 12,125 lb (5 500 kg); max landing weight, 11,023 lb (5 000 kg).

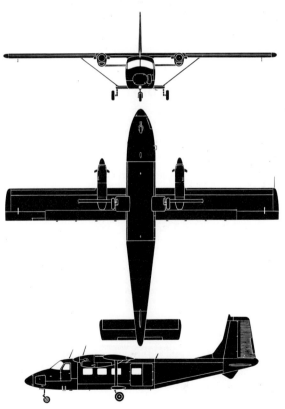

HAWKER SIDDELEY ARGOSY

Country of Origin: United Kingdom.

Type: Medium-range freighter and utility transport.

Power Plant: Four 2,230 shp (1 663 kW) Rolls-Royce Dart 532/1 turboprops.

Performance: (Srs 220): Max cruising speed, 282 mph (454 km/h) best economy cruise, 277 mph (446 km/h); range with max payload, 485 mls (780 km); range with max fuel, 1,760 mls (2 835 km).

Accommodation: Flight crew of two or three and space provision for up to 89 passengers.

Status: First AW 650 flown 8 January 1959; FAA certification (Srs 100) 2 December 1960 and first deliveries (Riddle Airlines) the same month. First Argosy Srs 200 flown 11 March 1964, entered service (BEA) February 1965.

Sales: Total of 17 Argosies built for commercial use; three Srs 100 and four Srs 200/220 in service early 1983.

Notes: The AW 650 Argosy was designed during the 'fifties by the former Armstrong Whitworth subsidiary of Hawker Siddeley as a specialized commercial freighter, but its principal market was found in the military rôle, for the RAF. Most of the initial production batch of Srs 100s served with Riddle Airlines on military charter operations in the USA and three of these have since returned to the UK to be operated by Air Bridge Carriers. The Srs 200/220 had structural refinements and uprated engines; for of the six built for BEA are still in service, two with IFEC Aviation in Australia and two with SAFE Air in New Zealand. The latter can be quickly fitted with 30-seat passenger modules when the aircraft are not carrying cargo.

HAWKER SIDDELEY ARGOSY 220

Dimensions: Span, 115 ft 0 in (33,05 m); length, 86 ft 9 in (26,44 m); height, 29 ft 3 in (8,91 m); wing area, 1,458 sq ft (135,45 m²).

Weights: Empty equipped, 48,920 lb (22 186 kg); max payload, 32,000 lb (14 515 kg); max fuel, 27,258 lb (12 364 kg); max zero fuel, 80,000 lb (36 288 kg); max take-off, 93,000 lb (42 185 kg); max landing, 88,500 lb (40 143 kg).

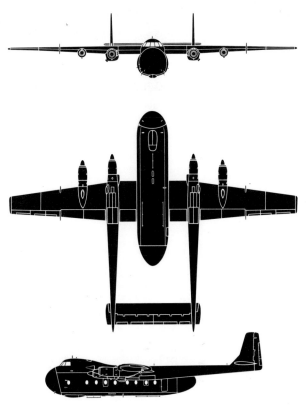

HAWKER SIDDELEY TRIDENT

Country of Origin: United Kingdom.
Type: Short/medium-range passenger transport.
Power Plant: Three 11,960 lb st (5 425 kgp) Rolls-Royce Spey 512-5W turbofans plus (Trident Three only) one 5,250 lb st (2 381 kgp) Rolls-Royce RB.162-86.
Performance: (Trident 2E): Typical high-speed cruise, 605 mph (972 km/h) at 27,000 ft (8 230 m); long-range cruise, 505 mph (812 km/h); range with max passenger payload, 2,430 mls (3 910 km); range with max fuel, 2,500 mls (4 025 km) with 16,020-lb (7 266-kg) payload.
Accommodation: Flight crew of three and up to 132 passengers six-abreast with central aisle, or 149 with some seat rows seven-abreast, at 28-in (71-cm) pitch.
Status: First Trident 1 flown 9 January 1962, entered service (BEA) 11 March 1964; first Trident 2E flown 27 July 1967, entered service (BEA) 18 April 1968. Trident Three first flown 11 December 1969, entered service (BEA) 1 April 1971. Production completed June 1978.
Sales: Total of 117 built, comprising 24 Srs 1, 15 Srs 1E, 50 Srs 2E; 26 Srs 3 and two Super 3B
Notes: Trident was developed to meet BEA requirements and principal sales were to BEA and to China's CAAC, which bought 33 Srs 2E and two Super 3B. The Srs 1, 1E and 2E had the same fuselage but different wing spans, fuel capacities and weights; Srs 3 had longer fuselage and jet boost engine in rear fuselage for higher operating weights. By 1983, British Airways (ex BEA) had retired most of its Trident 1s and some Trident 2Es; CAAC was still a major user of Trident 2Es.

HAWKER SIDDELEY TRIDENT 2E

Dimensions: Span, 98 ft 0 in (29,87 m); length, 114 ft 9 in (34,97 m); height, 27 ft 0 in (8,23 m); wing area, 1,462 sq ft (135,82 m).

Weights: Operating empty, 73,200 lb (33 203 kg); max payload 26,800 lb (12 156 kg); max fuel, 51,313 lb (23 275 kg); max zero fuel, 100,000 lb (45 360 kg); max take-off, 143,500 lb (65 090 kg); max landing, 113,000 lb (51 261 kg).

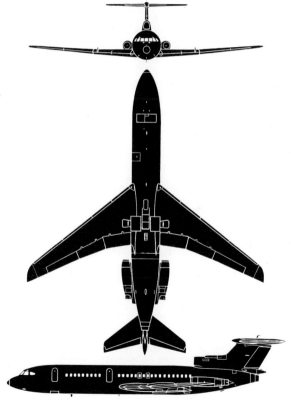

IAI 101B ARAVA

Country of Origin: Israel.
Type: Commuter airliner and general utility transport.
Power Plant: Two 750 shp (560 kW) Pratt & Whitney PT6A-36 turboprops.
Performance: Max cruise, 190 mph (306 km/h) at 10,000 ft (3050 m); long-range cruise, 183 mph (295 km/h) at 10,000 ft (3050 m); max payload range, 173 mls (278 km).
Accommodation: Crew of one or two and 18 passengers in four-abreast seating with central aisle.
Status: Two flying prototypes of the Arava commenced test on 27 November 1969 and 8 May respectively, certification as a civil aircraft being obtained in April 1972. Subsequent Arava production has been primarily of the military IAI 201, but the IAI 101B version was FAA-certificated on 17 November 1980, and this has since been marketed in the USA with the named of Cargo Commuterliner.
Sales: Customer deliveries of commercial model 101B commenced (to Key West Airlines) in 1981. Principal operator is Airspur, with a total fleet of 10.
Notes: The IAI 101B marketed in the USA as the Cargo Commuterliner, is a convertible passenger/cargo aircraft, the twin-boom configuration of this aircraft offering the advantage of straight-in rear loading through a full fuselage-width door. The Arava was originally conceived as a STOL utility transport primarily for military use and in this form has been supplied to more than a dozen armed services. One US operator, Airspur, which has purchased 10, flies passenger services with the IAI 101B by day and freight services by night.

IAI 101B ARAVA

Dimensions: Span, 68 ft 9 in (20,96 m); length, 42 ft 9 in (13,03 m); height, 17 ft 1 in (5,21 m); wing area, 470.2 sq ft (43,68 m²).

Weights: Operational empty, 8,818 lb (4 000 kg); max payload, 5,184 lb (2 351 kg); max zero fuel, 14,000 lb (6 350 kg); max take-off, 15,000 lb (6 804 kg); max landing, 15,000 lb (6 804 kg).

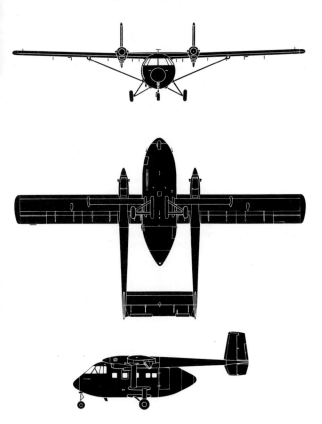

ILYUSHIN IL-18

Country of Origin: Soviet Union.

Type: Medium-range turboprop airliner.

Power Plant (Il-18E): Four 4,250 ehp (3 169 kW) Ivchenko AI-20M turboprops.

Performance (Il-18E): Max cruising speed, 419 mph (675 km/h); economical cruising speed, 388 mph (625 km/h); range with max payload, 1,990 mls (3 200 km); range with max fuel, 3,230 mls (5 200 km).

Accommodation: Normal flight crew of five (two pilots, flight engineer, navigator and radio operator). Standard accommodation for 110 passengers in two cabins six-abreast and a rear compartment five-abreast. Max accommodation, 122.

Status: Prototype 1I-18 first flown 4 July 1957; service use began (with Aeroflot) 20 April 1959. Production completed during 1968.

Sales: More than 600 Il-18s built, including approximately 100 exported to Communist Bloc countries in Europe, several African airlines, Cuba and China, and elsewhere.

Notes: A contemporary of the Antonov An-10, the Il-18 soon proved superior in the passenger-carrying rôle and in the two decades of the 'sixties and the 'seventies it played a major rôle in the expansion and modernisation of Aeroflot services within the Soviet Union and on international services in Europe and the Middle East. The 84-passenger Il-18V was the initial standard version, with 4,000 ehp (2 983 kW) AI-20K engines; the Il-18E (data above) had more power and a revised interior, and the Il-18D had increased fuel and a higher gross weight of 141,100 lb (64 000 kg).

ILYUSHIN IL-18E

Dimensions: Span, 122 ft 8½ in (37,40 m); length, 117 ft 9 in (35,9 m); height, 33 ft 4 in (10,17 m); wing area, 1,507 sq ft (140 m²).
Weights: Empty equipped, 76,350 lb (34 630 kg); max payload, 29,750 lb (13 500 kg); max take-off, 134,925 lb (61 200 kg).

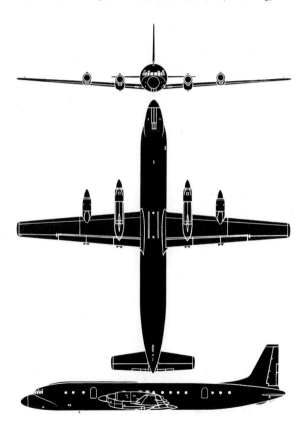

ILYUSHIN IL-62

Country of Origin: Soviet Union.
Type: Long-range jet transport.
Power Plant: Four (Il-62) 23,150 lb st (10 500 kgp); Kuznetsov NK-8-4 or (Il-62M) 24,250 lb st (11 000 kgp) Soloviev D-30KU turbofans.
Performance: (Il-62M): Typical cruising speed, 509–560 mph (820–900 km/h) at 35,000 ft (10 670 m); range with max payload, 4,846 mls (7 800 km); range with payload of 22,045 lb (10 000 kg), 6,215 mls (10 000 km).
Accommodation: Flight crew of five (two pilots, flight engineer, navigator and radio operator); maximum accommodation in two cabins for 186 passengers (174 in Il-62M, 195 in Il-62MK), six-abreast at a pitch of 34 in (86 cm) with central aisle.
Status: Prototype first flown January 1963 (with Lyulka AŁ-7 engines); service introduction (with Aeroflot) 15 September 1967. Il-62M first flown 1971 and entered service 1974; Il-62MK introduced 1978.
Sales: Approximately 100 for Aeroflot by 1982 and 40 for export, including CSA (8 plus 4 Il-62M), Interflug (7 plus 3 Il-62M), LOT (6 plus 5 Il-62M), Tarom (3 plus 2 Il-62M), Cubana (7 Il-62M) and CAAC (5).
Notes: The Il-62 was the first Soviet jetliner designed for long-range intercontinental operations. The original production version was powered by Kuznetsov NK-8-4 turbofans but the improved Il-62M, appearing in 1971, has Soloviev D-30s of greater thrust and lower specific fuel consumption, combined with a fin fuel tank for longer range. The Il-62MK has a higher gross weight (368,170 lb/167 000 kg), increasing payload to 195 passengers.

128

ILYUSHIN IL-62

Dimensions: Span, 141 ft 9 in (43,20 m); length, 174 ft 3½ in (53,12 m); height, 40 ft 6¼ in (12,35 m); wing area, 3,009 sq ft (279,55 m).

Weights: Operational weight empty, approximately 157,630 lb (71 500 kg); max payload, 50,700 lb (23 000 kg); max zero fuel, 208,550 lb (94 600 kg); max take-off, 363,760 lb (165 000 kg); max landing, 231,500 kg (105 000 kg).

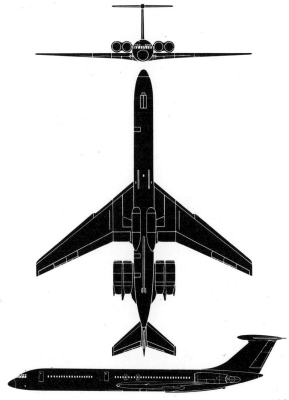

ILYUSHIN IL-76

Country of Origin: Soviet Union.
Type: Long-range military and civil freighter.
Power Plant: Four 26,455 lb st (12 000 kgp) Soloviev D-30KP turbofans.
Performance: Max level speed, 528 mph (850 km/h); typical cruise, 466–497 mph (750–800 km/h); range with max payload, 3,100 mls (5 000 km); max range, 4,163 mls (6 700 km).
Accommodation: Normal flight crew of five (two pilots, flight engineer, navigator, radio operator) plus two freight handlers. Pressurized main cabin, with freight handling equipment, can accomodate one, two or three 30-passenger self-contained modules.
Status: Prototype first flown 25 March 1971. Service use by Aeroflot began 1975.
Sales: About 40–50 Il-76T and Il-76M in service with Aeroflot by end of 1982; exports to Iraq (five T and three M), Libya (five T) and Syria (two T and two M). More than 100 aircraft in service with Soviet Transport Aviation force.
Notes: Development of this long-range freighter was put in hand in the late 'sixties to provide a replacement for the turboprop An-12, with greater capabilities. Like the Antonov aircraft, the Il-76 has military as well as commercial applications, but those flown by Aeroflot are used primarily to carry heavy supplies associated with engineering and construction activities in the more remote areas of the Soviet Union. Early production aircraft were designated Il-76T; a version called the Il-76M appeared subsequently and has internal and other changes, probably including higher operating weights.

130

ILYUSHIN IL-76T

Dimensions: Span, 165 ft 8 in (50,50 m); length, 152 ft 10½ in (46,59 m); height, 48 ft 5 in (14,76 m); wing area, 3,229.2 sq ft (300 m²).

Weights: Max payload, 88,185 lb (40 000 kg); max take-off weight, 374,785 lb (170 000 kg).

ILYUSHIN IL-86

Country of Origin: Soviet Union.

Type: Long-range jetliner.

Power Plant: Four 28,660 lb st (13 000 kgp) Kuznetsov NK-86 turbofans.

Performance: Typical cruising speed, 560–590 mph (900–950 km/h) at 35,000 ft (10 670 m); range with payload of 88,185 lb (40 000 kg), 2,235 mls (3 600 km); range with max fuel, 2,858 mls (4 600 km).

Accommodation: Normal flight crew of three (two pilots and flight engineer) plus provision for navigator. Maximum of 350 passengers, nine-abreast with two aisles; typical mixed class layout, 28 six-abreast in forward cabin and 206 eight-abreast in main and rear cabins.

Status: First of two prototypes flown at Moscow on 22 December 1976. First production-configured aircraft flown 24 October 1977. Proving flights began September 1978 and first scheduled service flown by Aeroflot 26 December 1980, and first international service (Moscow–East Berlin) 3 July 1981.

Sales: Ten in service with Aeroflot by February 1982, when production believed to be at a rate of 1–2 a month. First exports to LOT Polish Air Lines, 1983.

Notes: The Il-86 is the Soviet Union's first "airbus" type with a twin-aisle layout in the wide-body cabin; at first projected with a rear-engined layout, it was eventually built in the form illustrated after analyzing the structural weight penalties and low-speed handling difficulties of the latter. Major Il-86 airframe components are produced in Poland, and final assembly takes place at Voronezh in the USSR.

ILYUSHIN IL-86

Dimensions: Span, 157 ft 8¼ in (48,06 m); length, 195 ft 4 in (59,54 m); height, 51 ft 10½ in (15,81 m); wing area, 3,444 sq ft (320 m²).

Weights: Max payload, 92,600 lb (42 000 kg); max fuel load, 189,600 lb (86 000 kg); max take-off, 454,150 lb (206 000 kg); max landing, 385,800 lb (175 000 kg).

LET L-410

Country of Origin: Czechoslovakia.
Type: Light turboprop transport.
Power Plant: Two 730 ehp (544 kW) Walter M 601B turboprops.
Performance: Max cruise, 227 mph (365 km/h); economical cruise, 186 mph (300 km/h); range with max payload, 285 mls (460 km); range with max fuel, 646 mls (1 040 km).
Accommodation: Flight crew of two and 15 passengers three-abreast with off-set aisle at 30-in (76-cm) pitch.
Status: Prototype L-410 flown on 16 April 1969. First L-410M flown 1973. Prototype L-410 UVP flown 1 November 1977, certificated and entered service 1980. Production rate about eight a month by 1985.
Sales: Primary customer is Aeroflot, which had about 100 in service by early 1983.
Notes: Development of the L-410 light transport began at the Kunovice works of the Let National Corporation (Let Národni Podnik) in 1966, as the first complete aircraft project undertaken by that factory. The design is a conventional one for aircraft of its size but early development was delayed by non-availability of the M 601 turboprops, work on which was proceeding in parallel. The first 31 aircraft were completed as L-410As with Pratt & Whitney PT6A-27 engines and saw some service with CSA and Slov-Air, as did the L-410M with M-601 engines (110 built). The L-410 UVP is the definitive production version, adopted by Aeroflot for use on regional services; this has a slightly longer fuselage, dihedral on the tailplane and numerous other improvements. Aeroflot began regular operations with this version during 1981 and most production deliveries since then have been for the Soviet Union.

LET L-410 UVP

Dimensions: Span, 63 ft 10¾ in (19,48 m); length, 47 ft 5½ in (14,47 m); height, 19 ft 1½ in (5,83 m); wing area, 378.67 sq ft (35.18 m²).

Weights: Basic empty, 8,212 lb (3 725 kg); max payload, 2,888 lb (1 310 kg); max fuel, 2,205 lb (1 000 kg); max zero fuel, 11,398 lb (5 170 kg); max take-off, 12,566 lb (5 700 kg); max landing, 12,125 lb (5 500 kg).

LOCKHEED ELECTRA

Country of Origin: USA.
Type: Short-medium range passenger and cargo transport.
Power Plant: Four 3,750 ehp Allison 501-D13 turboprops.
Performance: Max cruise, 405 mph (652 km/h) at 22,000 ft (6 700 m); best economy cruise, 374 mph (602 km/h); range with max payload, 2,200 mls (3 540 km); range with max fuel, 2,500 mls (4 023 km).
Accommodation: Flight crew of two or three, and up to 98 passengers six-abreast at 38-in (96,5-cm) pitch.
Status: First of four development aircraft flown 6 December 1957, first production-standard aircraft flown 19 May 1958. Certification 22 August 1958, entered service (Eastern Airlines) 12 January 1959. Re-certification of modified aircraft 5 January 1961. Production completed.
Sales: Total production 170 including 55 L-188C version.
Notes: Electra was first airliner of US design and production with turbine power to enter commercial service, and proved to be the only large airliner of US origin to use turboprops. Basic variant was L-188A, and L-188C had extra fuel and was certificated for higher weights, being intended primarily for overwater operations. The early operational record of the Electra was marred by accidents caused by some structural deficiencies in the power plant mounting, eventually overcome by a modification programme and re-certification. About half of all Electras built remain in service, the majority of these having been converted for use as freighters, with large loading doors in the rear fuselage side, by such companies as Lockheed Aircraft Service and American Jet Industries.

LOCKHEED ELECTRA L-188A

Dimensions: Span, 99 ft 0 in (30,18 m); length, 104 ft 6 in (31,81 m); height, 32 ft 10 in (10.0 m); wing area, 1,300 sq ft (120,8 m²).

Weights: Empty equipped, 61,500 lb (27 895 kg); max payload, 22,825 lb (10 350 kg); max fuel, 37,500 lb (17 010 kg); max zero fuel, 86,000 lb (39 010 kg); max take-off, 116,000 lb (52 664 kg); max landing, 95,650 lb (43 387 kg).

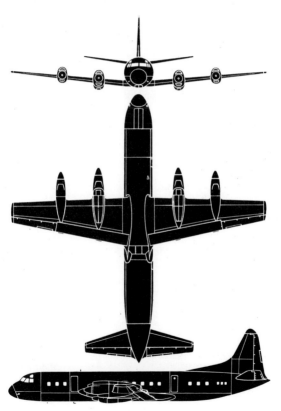

LOCKHEED L-100 HERCULES

Country of Origin: USA.
Type: Turboprop cargo transport.
Power Plant: Four, 4,508 ehp (3 362 kW) Allison 501-D22A turboprops.
Performance: Max cruise, 363 mph (583 km/h) at 20,000 ft (6 100 m); long-range cruise, 322 mph (579 km/h) (6000 m); range with max payload (-20), 2,417 mls (3 889 km), (-30), 2,005 mls (3 226 km); range with max fuel (zero payload) (-20), 4,891 mls (7 871 km), (-30), 4,833 mls (7 778 km).
Accommodation: Flight crew of three or four; usually all-freight configuration; provision for up to 91 passengers in quick-fit modules.
Status: Lockheed Model 382-44K-20 civil Hercules first flown 21 April 1964 and certificated 16 February 1965. L-100-20 first flown 19 April 1968, certificated 4 October 1968. L-100-30 first flown 14 August 1970, certificated 7 October 1970.
Sales: Approximately 90 L-100 commercial Hercules by 1983, within overall Hercules production of more than 1,700.
Notes: The L-100 designation applies to commercial models of the C-130 Hercules, although a few early examples were known by the Lockheed Model 382B designation. The early L-100s were dimensionally similar to the C-130, but the L-100-20 has the fuselage stretched by 8 ft 4 in (2,54 m) and the L-100-30 is longer by another 20 ft (6,1 m). A few L-100s have been bought as high-density low-cost passenger transports and Lockheed has projected a dedicated passenger-carrying version as well as further stretches, such as the L-100-50 with a total fuselage stretch of 36 ft 8 in (11,18 m) and higher gross weight.

LOCKHEED L-100-30

Dimensions: Span, 132 ft 7 in (40,41 m); length, 112 ft 9 in (34,37 m); height, 38 ft 3 in (11,66 m); wing area, 1,745 sq ft (162,12 m²).
Weights: Operating empty, 74,262 lb (33 684 kg); max payload, 50,738 lb (23 014 kg); max fuel, 46,462 lb (21.075 kg); max zero fuel, 127,000 lb (57 606 kg); max take-off, 155,000 lb (70 308 kg); max landing, 135,000 lb (61 236 kg).

LOCKHEED L-1011-100, -200 TRISTAR

Country of Origin: USA.

Type: Medium/long-range large-capacity airliner.

Power Plant: Three (-1, -100) 42,000 lb st (19 050 kgp) Rolls-Royce RB.211-22B or (-200) 50,000 lb st (22 680 kgp) RB.211-524 turbofans.

Performance (L-1011-200): Max cruising speed at mid-cruise weight, 605 mph (973 km/h) at 30,000 ft (9 145 m); economical cruising speed, 533 mph (890 km/h) at 35,000 ft (10 670 m); range with max passenger payload, 4,157 mls (6 690 km); range with max fuel, 5,661 mls (9 111 km).

Accommodation: Flight crew of three and up to 400 passengers 10-abreast with two aisles, at 30-in (76-cm) seat pitch; typical mixed-class, 256, basically nine-abreast.

Status: First L-1011 flown 17 November 1970 and fifth, completing the development batch, on 2 December 1971. Provisional certification 22 December 1971; full certification 14 April 1972 and first service (Eastern) 30 April. First flight with RB.211-524 engines, 12 August 1976; certification of -200 on 26 April 1977 and entered service with Saudia. Production completed 1984.

Sales: Total of 244 for 16 airlines (including L-1011-500, see next entry). Initial orders by Eastern Airlines and TWA; other operators of -1, -100 and -200 include Air Canada, Cathay Pacific, Gulf Air, Saudia, Delta and British Airways.

Notes: Lockheed launched the Tristar in March 1968 as the second of the wide-body transports. The -100 differs from the original -1 in having higher weights and more fuel, while the -200 is like the -100 but with uprated engines.

LOCKHEED L-1011-200 TRISTAR

Dimensions: Span, 155 ft 4 in (47,34 m); length, 177 ft 8½ in (54,17 m); height, 55 ft 4 in (16,87 m); wing area, 3,456 sq ft (320.0 m²).

Weights: Operating weight empty, 248,400 lb (112 670 kg); max payload, 89,600 lb (40 642 kg); max fuel weight, 176,930 lb (80 254 kg); max zero fuel, 338,000 lb (153 315 kg); max take-off, 466,000 lb (211 375 kg); max landing, 368,000 lb (166 920 kg).

141

LOCKHEED L-1011-500 TRISTAR

Country of Origin: USA.
Type: Long-range large-capacity airliner.
Power Plant: Three 50,000 lb st (22 680 kgp) Rolls-Royce RB.211-524B or B4 turbofans.
Performance: Max cruising speed at mid-cruise weight, 605 mph (973 km/h) at 30,000 ft (9 145 m); economical cruising speed, 553 mph (890 km/h) at 35,000 ft (10 670 m); range with max passenger payload, 6,025 mls (9 697 km); range with max fuel, 6,996 mls (11 260 km).
Accommodation: Flight crew of three and up to 330 passengers 10-abreast with two aisles at 30/33-in (76–83-cm) pitch; typical mixed class, 24F (six-abreast) and 222T (nine-abreast).
Status: First L-1011-500 flown 16 October 1978; extended wing-tips first flown (on original L-1011-1 prototype) in 1978 and on production -500 (with active ailerons) in November 1979. Entered service (British Airways, without active controls) 7 May 1979 and (Pan American, with active controls) early 1980. Certificated with fully-digital flight control system for Cat IIIA operations, 17 June 1981. Production completed 1984.
Sales: Ordered and/or operated by Aero Peru, Air Canada, Air Lanka, Alia, British Airways, BWIA, Delta, LTU, Pan American and TAP (Air Portugal).
Notes: The TriStar 500 was launched in August 1976 as a derivative of the -200 (see previous page), to provide a transport of longer range and reduced capacity. It features active controls to reduce wing bending moments, an improved wing-to-fuselage fairing and an advanced flight management system. Wing span is increased and fuselage length reduced.

142

LOCKHEED L-1011-500 TRISTAR

Dimensions: Span, 164 ft 4 in (50,09 m); length, 164 ft 2½ in (50,05 m); height, 55 ft 4 in (16,87 m); wing area, 3,540 sq ft (320,0 m²).

Weights: Operating weight empty, 245,400 lb (111 311 kg); max payload, 92,608 lb (42 006 kg); max fuel weight, 211,249 lb (95 821 kg); max zero fuel, 338,000 lb (153 315 kg); max take-off, 504,000 lb (228 610 kg); max landing, 368,000 lb (166 920 kg).

McDONNELL DOUGLAS DC-8

Country of Origin: USA.

Type: Long-range passenger and cargo transport.

Power Plant (Srs 50): Four 17,000 lb st (7945 kgp) Pratt & Whitney JT3D-1 or 18,000 lb st (8172 kgp) JT3D-3 turbofans.

Performance (Srs 50): Max cruise, 595 mph (958 km/h) at 25,000 ft (7620 m); best economy cruise, 544 mph (876 km/h) at 30,000 ft (9150 m); range with maximum payload, 4,700 mls (7560 km).

Accommodation: Flight crew of three and up to 179 passengers six-abreast with central aisle at 32-in (81-cm) pitch.

Status: First flights: Srs 10, 30 May 1958, Srs 20, 29 November 1958, Srs 30, 21 February 1959, Srs 40, 23 July 1959, Srs 50, 20 December 1960, Srs 55 Jet Trader, 20 October 1962, Srs 61, 14 March 1966, Srs 62, 29 August 1966; Srs 63, 10 April 1967. Certification: Srs 10, 31 August 1959; Srs 30, 1 February 1960; Srs 40, 24 March 1960; Srs 50, 10 October 1961; Srs 55 Jet Trader, 29 January 1963; Srs 61, 2 September 1966; Srs 62, 27 April 1967; Srs 63, 30 June 1967. Entry into service: Srs 10 (Delta, United) 18 September 1959; Srs 30 (Pan American) April 1960; Srs 40 (TCA) April 1960; Srs 61, 25 February 1967; Srs 62, 22 May 1967; Srs 63, 27 July 1967. Production completed, May 1972.

Sales: One prototype (unsold) and 555 DC-8s built, comprising 28 Srs 10, 24 Srs 20, 57 Srs 30, 32 Srs 40, 87 Srs 50, 54 Srs 55, 88 Srs 61, 68 Srs 62 and 107 Srs 63.

Notes: Srs 10 to 50 were dimensionally similar, with varying power plants, fuel capacity and weights; Srs 55 Jet Trader had cargo door. Srs 60 variants were larger—see next entry.

McDONNELL DOUGLAS DC-8 SERIES 50

Dimensions: Span, 142 ft 5 in (43,41 m); length, 150 ft 6 in (45,87 m); height, 42 ft 4 in (12,91 m); wing area, 2,868 sq ft (266,5 m²).

Weights: Empty equipped, 137,000 lb (62 143 kg); max payload, 46,500 lb (21 092 kg); max fuel, 156,180 lb (70 842 kg); max zero fuel, 183,500 lb (83 236 kg); max take-off, 315,000 lb (142 880 kg); max landing, 207,000 lb (93 900 kg).

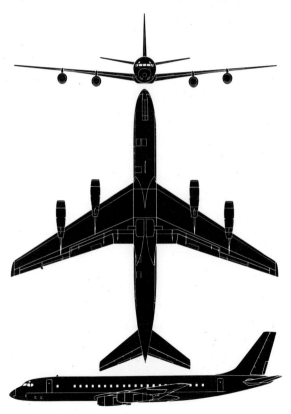

McDONNELL DOUGLAS DC-8 SERIES 70

Country of Origin: USA.

Type: Very long range turbofan transport.

Power Plant: Four 24,000 lb st (10 900 kgp) General Electric/SNECMA CFM56-2-1C turbofans.

Performance: Max speed, 600 mph (965 km/h); typical cruising speed, 531 mph (854 km/h) at 35,000 ft (10 670 m); max range with full passenger payload, (Srs 71) 4,650 mls (7482 km), (Srs 72) 7,215 mls (11 612 km), (Srs 73) 5,560 mls (8 945 km).

Accommodation: Flight crew of three and up to (Srs 71, 73) 269 or (Srs 72) 201 passengers six abreast with central aisle, at 30-in (76-cm) pitch.

Status: First Srs 71 conversion flown 15 August 1981; first Srs 72 flown 5 December 1981; first Srs 73 flown 4 March 1982. FAA certification (Srs 71) April 1982, entered service (Delta) 24 April and (United) 16 May.

Sales: Total of 94 conversions ordered by early 1983, plus about 40 options; principal airline customers are Delta, United, Overseas National, Flying Tiger, Trans America, Capitol, Air Canada, JAL, Spantax and Air Gabon.

Notes: The DC 8 Series 70 is a conversion of the Super Sixty series of DC-8s, with CFM56 turbofans replacing the original JT3D engines. Conversions are marketed by Cammacorp and made by McDonnell Douglas at Tulsa or at other sites, using kits. The designation Srs 71, 72 and 73 relate respectively to conversions of the Srs 61, 62 and 63; as data on the opposite page indicate, the Srs 72 has a shorter fuselage than the other two variants, while the Srs 72 and 73 have greater wing span then the Srs 71.

McDONNELL DOUGLAS DC-8 SERIES 70

Dimensions: Span, (Srs 71) 142 ft 5 in (43,40 m), (Srs 72, 73) 148 ft 5 in (45,23 m); length, (Srs 71,73) 187 ft 5 in (57,12 m), (Srs 72) 257 ft 5 in (47,98 m); height, (Srs 71, 73) 43 ft 0 in (13,1 m), (Srs 72) 43 ft 5 in (13,2 m); wing area, (Srs 71, 73) 2,884 sq ft (67,9 m²), (Srs 72) 2,927 sq ft (271,9 m²).

Weights (Srs 71): Operational empty, 156,000 lb (70 800 kg); max payload, 68,000 lb (30 850 kg); max fuel, 156,142 lb (70 825 kg); max zero fuel, 224,000 lb (101 600 kg); max take-off, 325,000 lb (147 400 kg); max landing, 240,000 lb (108 900 kg).

McDONNELL DOUGLAS DC-9 SRS 10–30

Country of Origin: USA.

Type: Short-range airliner.

Power Plant (Srs 30): Two 14,500 lb st (6 580 kgp) Pratt & Whitney JT8D-9 or 15,000 lb st (6 800 kgp) JT8D-11 or 15,500 lb st (7 030 kgp) JT8D-15 turbofans.

Performance (Srs 30): Max cruise, 579 mph (932 km/h) at 26,000 ft (7 925 m); long-range cruise, 496 mph (798 km/h) at 35,000 ft (10 670 m); range with 80-passenger payload, 1,923 mls (3 095 km); ferry range, max fuel, 2,280 mls (3 669 km).

Accommodation: Flight crew of two and up to 115 passengers five-abreast with offset aisle at 32-in (81-cm) pitch.

Status: First (Srs 10) development aircraft flown 25 February 1965; first Srs 30 flown 1 August 1966; first Srs 20 flown 18 September 1968. DC-9RF development aircraft (JT8D-109 engines) flown 9 January 1975. Certification: (Srs 10) 23 November 1965; (Srs 20), 11 December 1968; (Srs 30), 19 December 1966. Entry into service: Srs 10 (Delta), 8 December 1965; Srs 20 (SAS), 23 January 1969; Srs 30 (Eastern), 1 February 1967.

Sales: Total of 137 Srs 10 and 10 Srs 20 built; production complete. Approximately 670 Srs 30 sold to early 1983. Grand total of all variants (including military) sold (including options), 1,173, plus 35 for short-term lease.

Notes: Douglas launched the DC-9 in 1963 as a junior partner for the DC-8, and by 1980, the sales total had passed 1,000 (including the Srs 40, 50 and 80 variants described separately). The Srs 30 is the principal variant to date, 14 ft 11 in (4,6 m) longer than the Srs 10 and 20. Convertible (DC-9C) and freighter (DC-9F) versions are available.

McDONNELL DOUGLAS DC-9 SRS 30

Dimensions: Span, 93 ft 5 in (28,5 m); length, 119 ft 4 in (36,37 m); height, 27 ft 6 in (8,38 m); wing area, 1,001 sq ft (92,97 m²).

Weights: Operating weight empty, 57,190 lb (25 940 kg); max payload, 31,125 lb (14 118 kg); max fuel, 24,582 lb (11 150 kg); max zero fuel, 98,500 lb (44 678 kg); max take-off, 121,000 lb (54 885 kg); max landing, 110,000 lb (49 895 kg).

McDONNELL DOUGLAS DC-9 SRS 40–50

Country of Origin: USA.
Type: Short/medium range airliner.
Power Plant (Srs 50): Two 15,500 lb st (7030 kgp) Pratt & Whitney JT8D-15 or 16,000 lb st (7257 kgp) JT8D-17 turbofans.
Performance (Srs 50): Max cruise, 577 mph (929 km/h) at 27,000 ft (8230 m); long-range cruise, 507 mph (817 km/h) at 35,000 ft (10670 m); range with 97-passenger payload, 2,067 mls (3326 km); ferry range, max fuel, 2,516 mls (4049 km).
Accommodation: Flight crew of two and up to 139 passengers five-abreast, with offset aisle, at 31-in (79-cm) pitch.
Status: Srs 40 first flown on 28 November 1967, certificated 27 February 1968, entered service (SAS) 12 March 1968. Srs 50 first flown 17 December 1974; entered service (Swissair) 24 August 1975.
Sales: Total of 71 Srs 40 and over 100 Srs 50 sold by early 1983, with Srs 50 production continuing. Grand total of all variants sold (including options), 1,173.
Notes: The Srs 40 and Srs 50 represent two successive stages of fuselage "stretch", based on the DC-9 Srs 30 (see previous page), which remains the principal production variant. The Srs 40 is 6 ft 4 in (1,87 m) longer and was developed to meet a specific SAS requirement; only the Scandinavian airline and TDA in Japan have purchased this version as new-production aircraft from McDonnell Douglas. The Srs 50 had another 6 ft 4 in (1,87 m) added to the fuselage length and was developed in the first instance for Swissair. The Srs 50 in turn provided the basis for a number of further projected developments, from which the Srs 80 was chosen for production (see next page).

McDONNELL DOUGLAS DC-9 SRS 50

Dimensions: Span, 93 ft 5 in (28,47 m); length, 133 ft 7$\frac{1}{4}$ in (40,72 m); height, 28 ft 0 in (8,53 m); wing area, 1,001 sq ft (92,97 m²).

Weights: Operating weight empty, 61,880 lb (28 068 kg); max payload, 34,430 lb (15 617 kg); max fuel, 33,640 lb (15 259 kg); max zero fuel, 98,500 lb (44 400 kg); max take-off, 121,000 lb (54 900 kg); max landing, 110,000 lb (49 900 kg).

McDONNELL DOUGLAS DC-9 SUPER 80

Country of Origin: USA.

Type: Short/medium-range airliner.

Power Plant: Two (Super 81) 18,500 lb st (8400 kgp) Pratt & Whitney JT8D-209 turbofans with 750-lb st (340-kgp) reserve or (Super 82) 20,000 lb st (9072 kgp) JT8D-217 or -217A turbofans with 850-lb st (386-kgp) reserve.

Performance: Max cruise, 574 mph (924 km/h) at 27,000 ft (8230 m); long-range cruise, 505 mph (813 km/h) at 35,000 ft (10670 m); range with 137-passenger payload (Super 81) 2,014 mls (3241 km), (Super 82) 2,348 mls (3778 km); max fuel range (Super 81), 3,060 mls (4925 km), (Super 82) 2,990 mls (4812 km).

Accommodation: Flight crew of two and up to 172 passengers five-abreast, with off-set aisle, at 31-in (78-cm) seat pitch.

Status: Three development Super 81s first flown on 18 October 1979, 6 December 1979 and 29 February 1980; first Super 82 flown 8 January 1981. Super 81 certification on 25 August 1980; entry into service (Swissair) 5 October 1980. Super 82 certification July 1981, entry into service (Republic) August 1982.

Sales: Total of 232 Super 80s on order by early 1983, for 22 airlines. Grand total, all DC-9 variants, 1,173 including options, plus 35 Super 80s for short-term lease (to American and TWA).

Notes: The DC-9 Super 80 was launched in October 1977, as a "stretched" Srs 50 to take advantage of improved power plant. The Super 81 and Super 82 differ in engine power and operating weights; also certificated is a version with JT8D-217A engines and 149.5000-lb (67812-kg) gross weight. Projected Super 83 has a weight of 160,000 lb (72576 kg) and greater range.

McDONNELL DOUGLAS DC-9 SUPER 80

Dimensions: Span, 107 ft 10 in (32,87 m); length, 147 ft 10 in (45,06 m); height, 29 ft 8 in (9,03 m); wing area, 1,270 sq ft (118 m²).

Weights (Super 81): Operating empty, 79,757 lb (36 177 kg); max payload, 40,203 lb (18 236 kg); max fuel, 39,128 lb (17 748 kg); max zero fuel, 118,000 lb (53 524 kg); max take-off, 140,000 lb (63 500 kg); max landing, 128,000 lb (58 060 kg).

McDONNELL DOUGLAS DC-10

Country of Origin: USA.

Type: Medium/long-range large-capacity airliner.

Power Plant: Three (Srs 30) 49,000 lb st (22 226 kgp) General Electric CF6-50A or 51,000 lb st (23 134 kgp) CF6-50C or 52,500 lb st (23 814 kgp) CF6-50C1 or C2 turbofans or (Srs 40) 49,400 lb st (22 408 kgp) Pratt & Whitney JT9D-20 or 53,000 lb st (24 040 kgp) JT9D-59A turbofans.

Performance (Srs 30): Max cruise, 565 mph (908 km/h) at 30,000 ft (9 154 m); long-range cruise, 547 mph (880 km/h) at 31,000 ft (9 450 m); range with max payload, 4,606 mls (7 413 km); ferry range with max fuel, (zero playload) 7,490 mls (12 055 km).

Accommodation: Flight crew of three and up to 380 passengers ten-abreast with two aisles at 32-in (81-cm) seat pitch.

Status: First three development DC-10s (Srs 10s) flown 29 August, 24 October and 23 December 1970; certificated 29 July 1971, entered service (American Airlines) 5 August 1971. Srs 15 first flown 8 January 1981, certificated 12 June 1981, entered service with Aeromexico. Srs 30 first flown 21 June 1972, certificated 21 November 1972, entered scrvice with KLM and Swissair. Srs 30CF flown 28 February 1973, first deliveries (to TIA and ONA) April 1973. Srs 40 first flown 28 February 1972, certificated 20 October 1972, entered service with Northwest Orient.

Sales: Total of 366 commercial DC-10s sold, plus 60 KC-10A military tankers.

Notes: The DC-10 is the third Douglas jetliner. Srs 10 was US domestic version and Srs 30 is principal intercontinental version.

McDONNELL DOUGLAS DC-10 SRS 30

Dimensions: Span, 165 ft 4 in (40,42 m); length, 181 ft 7 in (55,35 m); height, 58 ft 1 in (17,7 m); wing area, 3,921 sq ft (364,3 m²).

Weights: Operating empty, 267,197 lb (121 198 kgp); max payload, 106,550 lb (48 330 kg); max fuel, 243,681 lb (110 532 kg); max zero fuel, 368,000 lb (166 922 kg); max take-off, 572,000 lb (259 450 kg); max landing, 403,000 lb (182 798 kg).

NAMC YS-11

Country of Origin: Japan.

Type: Short-range turboprop transport.

Power Plant: Two 3,060 shp (2 282 kW) Rolls-Royce Dart 542-10K turboprops.

Performance: Max cruising speed, 291 mph (469 km/h) at 15,000 ft (4 575 m); best economy cruise, 281 mph (452 km/h) at 20,000 ft (6 100 m); range with max payload (no reserves), 680 mls (1 090 km); range with max fuel (no reserve), 2,000 mls (3 215 km).

Accommodation: Flight crew of two or three and 60 passengers four-abreast with central aisle at 34-in (86-cm) pitch.

Status: Two prototypes flown on 30 August and 28 December 1962 respectively; first production YS-11 flown 23 October 1964; certification 25 August 1964, entered service (Toa Airways) April 1965. First YS-11A-200 flown 27 November 1967, certificated (by FAA) 3 April 1968. YS-11A-400 flown 17 September 1969. Production completed February 1974.

Sales: Production of the YS-11 totalled 182 (including prototypes), comprising 49 Srs 100, 95 Srs 200, 16 Srs 300, nine Srs 400, four Srs 500 and nine Srs 600; of the total, 23 sold initially to Japanese armed forces and remainder commercial. About 110 in commercial service early 1983.

Notes: The YS-11 was Japan's first post-war commercial transport to enter production, having been designed and built by a consortium made up of Mitsubishi, Kawasaki, Fuji, Shin Meiwa, Japan Aircraft Manufacturiing and Showa. The major users were, and still are in 1983, the Japanese domestic airlines TDA and All Nippon.

NAMC YS-11A-200

Dimensions: Span, 104 ft 11¾ in (32,00 m); length, 86 ft 3½ in (26,30 m); height, 29 ft 5½ in (8,98 m); wing area, 1,020.4 sq ft (94.8 m²).

Weights: Operating empty, 33,993 lb (15 419 kg); max payload, 14,508 lb (6 581 kg); max fuel, 12,830 lb (5 820 kg); max zero fuel, 48,500 lb (22 000 kg); max take-off, 54,010 lb (24 500 kg); max landing, 52,910 lb (24 000 kg).

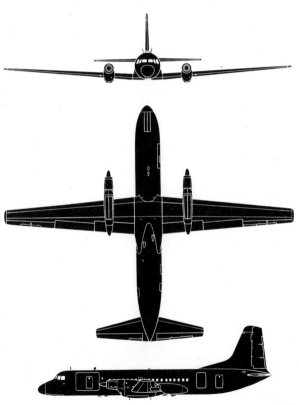

PILATUS BRITTEN-NORMAN ISLANDER

Country of Origin: United Kingdom.
Type: Light general purpose transport.
Power Plant: Two 260 hp (194 kW) Lycoming O-540-E4C5 or 300 hp (224 kW) Lycoming IO-540-K1B5 piston engines.
Performance (IO-540 engines): Max cruise, 164 mph (264 km/h) at 7,000 ft (2 135 m); economical cruise, 152 mph (245 km/h); range, 639–706 mls (1 028–1 136 km) with standard fuel, 940–1,042 mls (1 513–1 677 km) with auxiliary fuel.
Accommodation: Pilot and up to nine passengers in pairs with no aisle.
Status: Prototype BN-2 flown 13 June 1965 with Continental IO-360 engines and 17 December 1965 with O-540 engines, second prototype flown 20 August 1966. First production Islander flown 24 April 1967; certification 10 August 1967 with first delivery 13 August (Glosair). First flown with IO-540 engines 30 April 1970 and with TIO-540 engines 30 April 1971. BN-2S (long-nosed) flown 22 August 1972. Turbo-Islander prototype (Lycoming LTP101 engines) flown 6 April 1977; BN-2T Turbine Islander (Allison 250 engines) flown 2 August 1980, certificated mid-1981, first deliveries 1982.
Sales: Over 1,000 Islanders of all variants (including military Defenders) sold by early 1983.
Notes: The Islander is used for a variety of tasks including air taxi and some scheduled services. Basic model has 260 hp piston engines and optional model has 300 hp; both are available with extra fuel and extended wing tips. Turboprop version was introduced in 1981 and sales of this version were accelerating following US certification on 15 July 1982.

158

PILATUS BRITTEN-NORMAN ISLANDER

Dimensions: Span, 49 ft 0 in (14,94 m); span, fuel tanks in wing tips, 53 ft 0 in (16,15 m); height, 13 ft 8¾ in (4,18 m); wing area, 325.0 sq ft (30,19 m²); wing area, extended tips, 337.0 sq ft (31,31 m²).

Weights: Empty equipped, 3,738 lb (1 695 kg); max zero fuel weight, 6,300 lb (2 855 kg); max take-off and landing, 6,600 lb (2 993 kg).

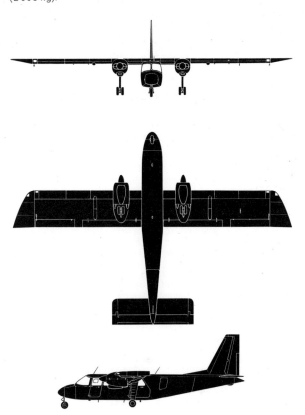

PILATUS BRITTEN-NORMAN TRISLANDER

Country of Origin: United Kingdom.
Type: Commuter airliner and general utility transport.
Power Plant: Three 260 hp (194 kW) Avco Lycoming O-540-E4C5 piston engines.
Performance (BN2A Mk III-2): Max cruise, 166 mph (267 km/h) at 8,000 ft (2 438 m); long-range cruise, 150 mph (241 km/h) at 8,000 ft (2 438 m); max payload range (with 3,600 lb/1 633 kg), 150 m|s (241 km).
Accommodation: Flight crew of one or two and up to 17 passengers at 29-in (74-cm) pitch two-abreast with no aisle; access to seats through individual doors.
Status: Prototype first flown 11 September 1970; first production aircraft flown 6 March 1971 followed by certification on 14 May 1971. First customer delivery (Aurigny Air Services, Jersey) 29 June 1971.
Sales: Seventy-three Trislanders delivered and in service by end-1982. Production transferred to USA in 1982/83.
Notes: The Trislander originated as a three-engined, lengthened-fuselage version of the Islander. It has sold in only relatively small numbers (compared with more than 1,000 Islanders) and production in the UK was temporarily suspended in 1982, although the Trislander was still being actively promoted for the commuter market. In the USA, it is marketed by International Aviation Corporation as the Tri-Commutair; this company purchased complete sets of components to permit assembly of about 20 Tri-Commutairs at its plant near Miami, starting late 1983, and IAC also has a licence for further Trislander/Tri-Commutair production in 1984.

160

PILATUS BRITTEN-NORMAN TRISLANDER

Dimensions: Span, 53 ft 0 in (16,15 m); length, 49 ft 2½ in (15,00 m); height, 14 ft 2 in (4,32 m); wing area, 337 sq ft (31,30 m²).

Weights: Operational empty, 5,843 lb (2 650 kg); max payload, 3,600 lb (1 633 kg); max zero fuel, 9,700 lb (4 400 kg); max take-off and landing, 10,000 lb (4 536 kg).

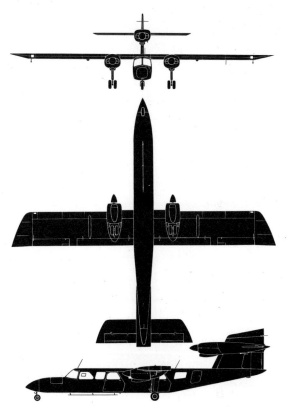

PIPER T-1040

Country of Origin: USA.
Type: Light turboprop commuter liner.
Power Plant: Two 500 shp (373 kW) Pratt & Whitney PT6A-11 turboprops.
Performance: Max cruising speed, 240 mph (376 km/h) at sea level and 274 mph (441 km/h) at 11,000 ft (3 353 m); range with max payload, 450 mls (724 km) at 10,000 ft (3 050 m); range with nine passengers, 770 mls (1 240 km).
Accommodation: Eleven individual seats in cabin, including one or two pilot's seats side-by-side.
Status: Prototype T-1040 first flown 17 July 1981, certificated early March 1982. Deliveries began (T-1040) April 1982, (T-1020) December 1981.
Sales: Totals not reported; early users include Atlantis Airlines (T-1040) and Astec Air East (T-1020).
Notes: Piper Aircraft Corp set up an Airline Division in June 1981, and at the same time announced two new aircraft for commuter use. One, the T-1020, is essentially the same as the PA-31-350 Navajo Chieftain, several hundred of which were already in commuter operation (see photo); it has Lycoming IO-540 piston engines, a special interior to airline standards and reduced fuel capacity to permit a greater payload to be carried, including baggage in an extended nose compartment. The T-1040 has basically the same fuselage as the T-1020, married to nose, wings and tail unit of the PA-31T-1 Cheyenne 1, including the latter's PT6A-11 turboprop engines. Several other Piper Twins are in commuter airline/air taxi use, including the T-tailed Cheyenne III and the smaller Aztec and Seneca.

162

PIPER T-1040

Dimensions: Span, 41 ft 1 in (12,52 m); length, 36 ft 8 in (11,18 m); height, 12 ft 9 in (3,89 m); wing area, 229 sq ft (21,27 m²).

Weights: Standard empty weight, 5,230 lb (2372 kg); useful load, 3,820 lb (1733 kg); cabin load with full fuel, 1,810 lb (820 kg); max fuel, 1,283 lb (582 kg); max zero fuel, 7,600 lb (3447 kg); max take-off and landing, 9,000 lb (4082 kg).

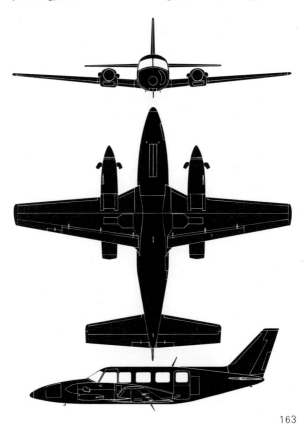

SAAB-FAIRCHILD 340

Country of Origin: Sweden and USA.
Type: Regional airliner.
Power Plant: Two 1,675 eshp (1250 kW) General Electric CT7-5A turboprops.
Performance: Max cruise, 300 mph (482 km/h) at 15,000 ft (4 570 m) at 25,000 lb (11 340 kg) gross weight; max payload range (34 passengers), at least 920 mls (1 480 km).
Accommodation: Flight crew of two with provision for third crew member and 34 passengers at 30-in (76-cm) pitch three-abreast with offset aisle.
Status: First of two flying prototypes rolled out on 27 October 1982, with flight test commencing on 25 January 1983. Certification scheduled for March 1984, with first customer delivery (to Crossair) in following month. Current planning calls for 24 to be delivered by end of 1984, with 50 being completed in 1985, 63 in 1986, and peak annual production of 72 aircraft being achieved in 1987.
Sales: By the end of 1982 firm orders had been recorded for 80 of these airliners divided between Europe (25), Middle East (five), Asia/Australasia (18), Latin America (four) and North America (28), plus 25 of the corporate version.
Notes: Saab-Fairchild is a partnership between Saab-Scania (Sweden) and Fairchild Industries (USA), established by an agreement signed on 25 January 1980, to develop the Model 340 regional airliner on a 50–50 basis. Fuselage construction and final assembly are undertaken in Sweden, with wings built by Fairchild at San Antonio; aircraft for North and Central America also are furnished and finished in the USA.

SAAB-FAIRCHILD 340

Dimensions: Span, 70 ft 4 in (21,44 m); length, 64 ft 8 in (19,72 m); height, 22 ft 6 in (6,87 m); wing area, 450 sq ft (41,80 m²).

Weights: Operational empty, 15,860 lb (7 194 kg); max payload, 7,140 lb (3 239 kg); max zero fuel, 23,000 lb (10 433 kg); max take-off, 26,000 lb (11 794 kg); max landing, 25,500 lb (11 567 kg).

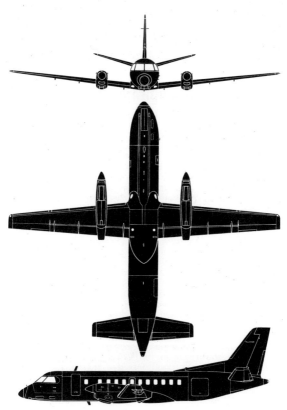

SHANGHAI Y-10

Country of Origin: China.
Type: Medium-range jet transport.
Power Plant: Four 19,000 lb st (8 618 kgp) Pratt & Whitney JT3D-7 turbofans.
Performance: Max speed, 605 mph (974 km/h); max cruising speed, 570 mph (917 km/h); range with max 178-passenger payload, 3,400 mls (5 470 km).
Accommodation: Flight crew of three or four. Standard layout provides 178 passenger seats six-abreast with central aisle at 32-in (81-cm) pitch.
Status: First prototype flown late summer of 1980; first reported cross-country flight (Shanghai to Peking) made on 8 December 1981.
Sales: No details available. Intended to meet needs of CAAC for domestic and international service.
Notes: China's aircraft industry, with major development centres in several towns including Shanghai, has been engaged for a number of years in an effort to bring its resources and capabilities up to Western standards. One of the most important projects in the furtherance of this objective was the design and construction of this four-engined jet transport, in a similar class as the Boeing 707. The first flight was made about 10 years after the project was launched, and was materially aided by the availability of JT3D engines purchased as spares for CAAC's fleet of Boeing 707s acquired from the USA. It is clear that the design has been influenced by that of the Boeing 707, although it is somewhat smaller, and the Y-10 should not be regarded simply as a "Chinese copy" of the US airliner.

SHANGHAI Y-10

Dimensions: Span, 138 ft 7 in (42,24 m); length, 140 ft 10¼ in (42,93 m); height, 44 ft 0½ in (13,42 m); wing area, 2,632.9 sq ft (244,6 m²).
Weights: Typical operating empty, 175,397 lb (79 560 kg); normal payload, 47,180 lb (21 400 kg); max payload, 52,250 lb (23 700 kg); max take-off, 224,870 lb (102 000 kg); max landing, 189,600 lb (86 000 kg).

SHORT BELFAST

Country of Origin: United Kingdom.
Type: Heavy duty freighter.
Power Plant: Four 5,730 shp Rolls-Royce Tyne RTy 12 turboprops.
Performance: Max cruise, 352 mph (566 km/h) at 24,000 ft (7 300 m); typical cruise, 316 mph (510 km/h); range with max payload, about 975 mls (1 575 km); range with 22,000-lb (10 000-kg) payload, 3,855 mls (6 200 km).
Accommodation: Flight crew of three or four. All-freight payload, with provision for up to 19 passengers on upper deck.
Status: First of 10 Belfast C Mk 1s for RAF flown 5 January 1964; deliveries began 20 January 1966. Certificated 6 March 1980 for commercial service starting same month.
Sales: Total of 10 aircraft built for RAF, in service until September 1976. Five acquired ex-RAF by Eurolatin 1977 for civil conversion, of which three operated by TAC Heavylift (now Heavylift) with two in reserve in 1983.
Notes: The massive Belfast was developed to a specific RAF requirement for a long-range strategic freighter but was withdrawn from service after 10 years. For commercial operation by Heavylift (a subsidiary of the Trafalgar House group), Marshall of Cambridge designed and made a number of modifications to improve the low-speed control and to bring systems and equipment in general into line with contemporary civil standards. Of five aircraft available for conversion, three were in service by 1981, and have found a number of useful applications world-wide as a result of their large capacity with straight-in-loading through the rear door.

SHORT BELFAST

Dimensions: Span, 158 ft 10 in (48,41 m); length, 136 ft 5 in (41,58 m); height, 47 ft 0 in (14,33 m); wing area, 2,466 sq ft (229,09 m²).

Weights: Typical operating weight empty, 130,000 lb (58 967 kg); max payload, 75,000 lb (34 000 kg); fuel load, 82,400 lb (37 376 kg); max zero fuel, 205,000 lb (92 986 kg); max take-off, 230,000 lb (104 325 kg); max landing, 215,000 lb (97 520 kg).

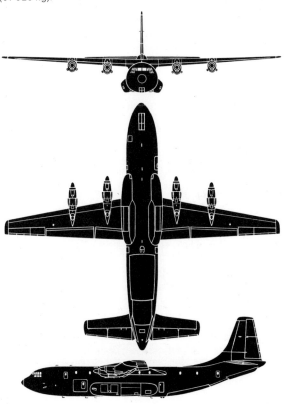

SHORTS SKYVAN

Country of Origin: United Kingdom.
Type: Short-range general utility transport.
Power Plant: Two 715 shp (533 kW) Garrett TPE331-201
turboprops.
Performance: Max cruise, 203 mph (327 km/h) at 10,000 ft
(3050 m); economical cruise, 173 mph (278 km/h) at 10,000 ft
(3050 m); range, 694 mls (1115 km); range with max freight
payload, 187 mls (300 km).
Accommodation: Flight crew of one or two and up to 19
passengers seated two abreast with centre aisle at 29-in (74-cm)
pitch.
Status: Prototype first flown (with piston engines) 17 January
1963 and (with Astazou turboprops) 2 October 1963. First Srs II
flown 29 October 1965; first Srs 3 flown 15 December 1967,
entered commercial service mid-1968.
Sales: Total production, approximately 150 by early 1983,
including 19 Srs II and 54 Srs 3M (military).
Notes: The Skyvan was developed as a utility transport for
military or civil use, and first flew with Continental piston engines.
Turboprops were substituted before the type entered production
and the Garrett TPE331 was adopted after a small initial batch
had been built with Astazou engines. The rear loading ramp makes
the Skyvan attractive to operators wishing to carry freight or
mixed loads and most examples have been delivered with rapidly
convertible interiors. The Skyvan was among the first small
turboprop transport to enter third-level airline service (now usually
called regional airline operations) and provided the basis for
development of the larger Shorts 330 and 360.

170

SHORTS SKYVAN SERIES 3

Dimensions: Span, 64 ft 11 in (19,79 m); length (including optional nose radome) 41 ft 0 in (12,50 m); height, 15 ft 1 in (4,60 m); wing area, 373 sq ft (34,65 m²).

Weights: Operating empty, 8,100 lb (3 674 kg); max payload, 4,600 lb (2 086 kg); max fuel, 3,126-lb (1 418 kg); max take-off, 12,000 lb (5 670 kg); max landing, 12,500 lb (5 670 kg).

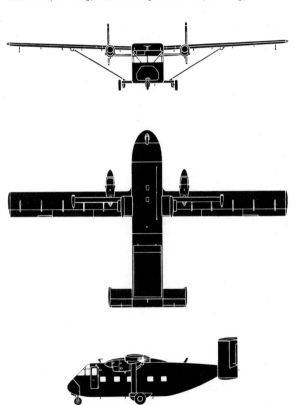

SHORTS 330

Country of Origin: United Kingdom.
Type: Regional airliner.
Power Plant: Two (330–100) 1,173 shp (875 kW) Pratt & Whitney PT6A-45B or (330-200) 1,198 shp (893 kW) PT6A-45R turboprops.
Performance (330–200): Max cruise, 219 mph (352 km/h) at 10,000 ft (3 050 m); long-range cruise, 183 mph (294 km/h) at 10,000 ft (3 050 m); max payload range, 550 mls (885 km).
Accommodation: Flight crew of two and 30 passengers at 30-in (76-cm) pitch three-abreast with offset aisle.
Status: Engineering prototype (SD3-30) flown on 22 August 1974, with production prototype following on 8 July 1975. First production aircraft flown 15 December 1975, first customer deliveries mid-1976, entry into service (Time Air, Canada) 24 August 1976. The 330-200 was announced mid-1981.
Sales: One hundred and eleven orders and options had been placed for the Shorts 330 by beginning of 1983, for 34 operators in 14 countries, with 86 aircraft delivered. Production continuing in parallel with Shorts 360.
Notes: As the SD3-30, the Shorts 330 was evolved from the Skyvan, with same fuselage cross section but lengthened, and with greater wing span. Original gross weight was 22,690 lb (10 250 kg) with PT6A-45 engines. The 330-200 incorporates a number of product improvements, having similar engines to those of the 360 permitting elimination of the water-methanol system of the -100 and featuring as standard several items previously listed as options. The name Sherpa is used for a version with rear-loading door and ramp for cargo operations.

SHORTS 330

Dimensions: Span, 74 ft 8 in (22,76 m); length, 58 ft 0½ in (17,69 m); height, 16 ft 3 in (4,95 m); wing area, 453 sq ft (42,10 m²).

Weights (330-200): Operational empty, 14,764 lb (6 697 kg); max payload (passenger), 5,850 lb (2 655 kg); max payload (freight), 7,500 lb (3 400 kg); max take-off, 22,900 lb (10 387 kg); max landing, 22,600 lb (10 251 kg).

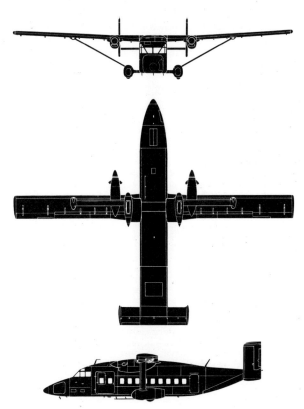

SHORTS 360

Country of Origin: United Kingdom.
Type: Regional airliner.
Power Plant: Two flat-rated 1,198 shp (893 kW) Pratt & Whitney PT6A-45R turboprops.
Performance: Max cruise, 242 mph (390 km/h) at 10,000 ft (3 050 m); long-range cruise, 198 mph (318 km/h) at 10,000 ft (3 050 m); max payload range (36 passengers), 500 mls (805 km).
Accommodation: Flight crew of two and 36 passengers at 30-in (76-cm) pitch three-abreast with offset aisle.
Status: Prototype first flown on 1 June 1981; first production 360 flown 19 August 1982 with certification on 3 September, and first customer delivery (to Suburban Airlines of Pennsylvania) following US certification in November.
Sales: By beginning of 1983 orders and options totalled 36 aircraft from 12 operators in four countries (including five operators in the USA).
Notes: Essentially a growth version of the Shorts 330 (see previous page) the 360 differs from its progenitor primarily in having a 3-ft (91-cm) cabin stretch ahead of the wing and an entirely redesigned rear fuselage and tail assembly. These changes allow cabin capacity to be increased by two seat rows and result in lower aerodynamic drag which contributes to a higher perfor-mance. Like the 330, the 360 is unpressurized and is being produced alongside the earlier regional airliner, which remains somewhat less expensive and therefore of interest to some operators who do not object to the Skyvan-type rear fuselage and tail unit and do not require the extra seating capacity that the 360 offers.

SHORTS 360

Dimensions: Span, 74 ft 8 in (22,75 m); length, 70 ft 6 in (21,49 m); height, 22 ft 7 in (6,88 m); wing area, 453 sq ft (42,10 m²).
Weights: Operational empty, 16,490 lb (7 480 kg); max payload, 7,020 lb (3 185 kg); max take-off, 25,700 lb (11 657 kg); max landing, 25,400 lb (11 521 kg).

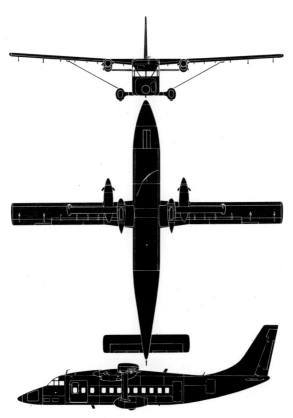

TRANSALL C-160

Country of Origin: France and Germany.
Type: Military freighter and special purpose transport.
Power Plant: Two 6,100 ehp (4 599 kW) Rolls-Royce Tyne R.Ty 30 Mk 22 turboprops.
Performance: Max speed, 319 mph (513 km/h) at 16,000 ft (4 875 m); max cruise, 311 mph (500 km/h); range with max payload, 1,151 mls (1 853 km); range with 17,690-lb (8 000-kg) payload, 3,160 mls (5 095 km).
Accommodation: Flight crew of three (including flight engineer). Space provided for up to 93 passengers.
Status: Prototype (C-160 VI) first flown 25 February 1963 (in France); C-160 V2 flown 25 May 1963 and C-160 V3 on 19 February 1964 (both in Germany). First (of six) pre-production C-160A flown 21 May 1965. First delivery (military) 2 August 1967. Civil certification 22 June 1973 (for Air France/Aéropostale). First new-series Transall flown 9 April 1981. First delivery (commercial for Indonesia) 9 February 1982.
Sales: Total production, first series, three prototypes, six pre-production, and 169 for France, Germany and South Africa, of which four to Air France. Twenty-eight new series on order early 1983 of which three for Indonesian Government.
Notes: The Transall was conceived to meet the needs of the French and German air forces for a tactical transport and was designed and produced as a joint venture. Four of the French aircraft were diverted to Air France for its Aéropostale overnight mail delivery service within France. Three aircraft from the second production batch were purchased by the Indonesian Government for its transmigration scheme.

TRANSALL C-160

Dimensions: Span, 131 ft 3 in (40,00 m); length, 106 ft 3½ in (32,40 m); height, 38 ft 2¾ in (11,65 m); wing area, 1,722 sq ft (160,0 m²).

Weights: Typical operating weight empty, 63,935 lb (29 000 kg); max payload, 35,275 lb (16 000 kg); max zero fuel, 99,210 lb (45 000 kg); max take-off, 112,435 lb (51 000 kg); max landing, 103,615 lb (47 000 kg).

TUPOLEV TU-134

Country of Origin: Soviet Union.
Type: Short/medium-range jetliner.
Power Plant: Two 14,990 lb st (6 800 kgp) Soloviev D-30 Srs II turbofans.
Performance (Tu-134A): Max cruise, 550 mph (885 km/h) at 32,800 ft (10 000 m) at weight of 92,600 lb (42 000 kg); long-range cruise, 466 mph (750 km/h); range with max payload, 1,174 mls (1 890 km); range with payload of 11,025 lb (5 000 kg), 1,876 mls (3 020 km).
Accommodation: Flight crew of three (two pilots and a navigator). Max one-class layout, 86 passengers; typical mixed class accommodation, 12 plus 56, all four-abreast with central aisle.
Status: Prototype testing began late 1962, with five more aircraft flown 1963/64. Full commercial service began (with Aeroflot) September 1967 on Moscow–Stockholm route. Tu-134A entered service 1970.
Sales: At least 200 for Aeroflot and about 100 for export to the East European airlines and Yugoslavia.
Notes: The Tu-134 emerged at about the same time as such Western types as the BAC One-Eleven and McDonnell Douglas DC-9, with which it shared a similar rear-engined T-tailed layout, and was the Tupolev design bureau's first wholly-original design for commercial use. The Tu-134A differs from the original model in having the fuselage lengthened by 6 ft 10½ in (2,10 m) and improved equipment; further improvements were planned for the Tu-134B-1, which was reported to be under development in the Soviet Union in 1982.

TUPOLEV TU-134A

Dimensions: Span, 95 ft 1¾ in (29,00 m); length, 121 ft 6½ in (37,05 m); height, 30 ft 0 in (9,14 m); wing area, 1,370.3 sq ft (127,3 m²).

Weights: Operating weight empty, 64,045 lb (29 050 kg); max payload, 18,075 lb (8 200 kg); max fuel weight, 31,800 lb (14 400 kg); max take-off, 103,600 lb (47 000 kg); max landing, 94,800 lb (43 000 kg).

TUPOLEV TU-154

Country of Origin: Soviet Union.
Type: Medium-range jetliner.
Power Plant: Three (Tu-154) 20,950 lb st (9 500 kgp) Kuznetsov NK-8-2 or (Tu-154A and B) 23,150 lb st (10 500 kgp) NK-8-2U turbofans.
Performance (Tu-154B): Typical cruising speed, 560–590 mph (900–950 km/h) at 36,000 ft (10 975 m); range with max payload, 1,865 mls (3 000 km); range with 164 passengers plus baggage, 2,175 mls (3 500 km).
Accommodation: Normal flight crew of three (two pilots and flight engineer) plus provision for navigator. Typical one-class layouts for 146 passengers six-abreast at 32-in (81-cm) pitch or 167-169 at 29.5-in (75-cm) pitch; mixed class layout for 12 first-class and 128 tourist class.
Sales: First of six prototype/development Tu-154s flown on 4 October 1968. Early route-proving flights with Aeroflot began May 1971. First regular commercial service began within Soviet Union 9 February 1972 and first international service (Moscow–Prague) 1 August 1972. In production (Tu-154B) 1982.
Sales: More than 300 delivered to Aeroflot and up to 50 for export to Balkan Bulgarian (16), Cubana (4), Malev (9), Tarom (11) and Alyemda.
Notes: The Tu-154 emerged in 1966, featuring a particularly good air-field performance and ability to operate from rough fields. The Tu-154A and Tu-154B are progressive improvements of the original Tu-154, and the Tu-154B-2 has imported French flight control and navaid equipment for Cat II operations. A variant with Soloviev D-30 engines under development is designated Tu-164.

TUPOLEV TU-154B

Dimensions: Span, 123 ft 2½ in (37,55 m); length, 157 ft 1¾ in (47,90 m); height, 37 ft 4¾ in (11,40 m); wing area, 2,169 sq ft (201,45 m²).

Weights: Basic operating, 111,940 lb (50 775 kg); max payload, 41,887 lb (19 000 km); max fuel load, 87,633 lb (39 750 lb); max zero fuel weight, 156,525 lb (71 000 kg); max take-off, 216,050 lb (98 000 kg); max landing, 171,960 lb (78 000 kg).

VICKERS VISCOUNT

Country of Origin: United Kingdom.
Type: Short-range turboprop transport.
Power Plant: Four 2,100 ehp (1 566 kW) Rolls-Royce Dart 525 turboprops.
Performance (V.810): Typical crusing speed, 350 mph (563 km/h) at 20,000 ft (6 100 m); range with max (64-passenger) payload, 970 mls (1 560 km); range with max fuel, 1,010 mls (1 625 km).
Accommodation: Flight crew of two or three and up to 69 passengers five-abreast with off-set aisle, at 34-in (86-cm) pitch.
Status: V.630 prototype for Viscount series first flown 16 July 1948; V.700 flown 19 April 1950; first production V.701 flown 20 August 1952, certificated 17 April 1953 and entered service (BEA) 18 April. V.800 prototype flown 27 July 1956, first delivery (V.802 for BEA) 11 January 1957. V.810 prototype flown 23 December 1957. Production completed 1964.
Sales: Total of 438 Viscounts sold, plus six prototypes and unsold demonstrators. Major fleet buyers were BEA, TCA and Capital Airlines. About 70 Viscounts in airline service in 1983, plus others as executive transports.
Notes: The Viscount was the world's first turboprop airliner, entering service almost a year after the de Havilland Comet had become the world's first turbojet transport. The Viscount was also to prove the best-selling commercial transport of all-British design and production. The V.700 and V.800 variants differ in fuselage length, power and weights; individual customer variants within each series had identifying designations with "7" or "8" prefixes as appropriate.

VICKERS VISCOUNT V.810

Dimensions: Span, 93 ft 8½ in (28,50 m); length, 85 ft 8 in (26,11 m); height, 26 ft 9 in (8,16 m); wing area, 963 sq ft (89,46 m²).

Weights: Basic operating, 41,565 lb (18 753 kg); max payload, 14,500 lb (6 577 kg); max fuel weight, 15,609 lb (7 080 kg); max zero fuel, 57,500 lb (26 082 kg); max take-off, 72,500 lb (32 886 kg); max landing, 62,000 lb (28 123 kg).

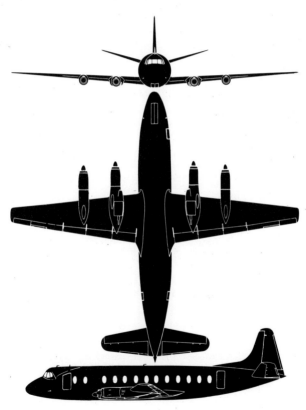

VICKERS VANGUARD

Country of Origin: United Kingdom.

Type: Short- to medium-range turboprop airliner.

Power Plant: Four 5,545 eshp (4 135 kW) Rolls-Royce Tyne 512 turboprops.

Performance: High speed cruise, 425 mph (684 km/h) at 20,000 ft (6 100 m); long-range cruise, 420 mph (676 km/h) at 25,000 ft (7 620 m); range with max payload, 1,380 mls (2 220 km); range with max fuel and 20,000-lb (9 080-kg) payload, 2,600 mls (4 185 km).

Accommodation: Flight crew of two or three and up to 139 passengers at 34-in (86-cm) pitch, seated six-abreast with central aisle.

Status: Prototype (V.950) flown 20 January 1959; first production V.951 flown 22 April 1959; certificated 2 December 1960, entered service (BEA) 17 December 1960. First V.952 flown 21 May 1960, entered service (TCA) 1 February 1961. First V.953 flown 1 May 1961.

Sales: One prototype; six V.951 and 14 V.953 for BEA and 23 V.952 for TCA.

Notes: The Vanguard was evolved as an enlarged-capacity successor for the Viscount, but it was overtaken by the first of the short-haul pure jet transports and sales totalled only 43. Twelve of BEA's Vanguards were later converted to V.953C Merchantman standard with cargo loading door in forward fuselage side and cargo handling facilities. Vanguards sold by BEA and TCA (now Air Canada) were acquired by several smaller operators in Europe and Indonesia, and fewer than a dozen of these remained in service by the end of 1982.

VICKERS VANGUARD V.953

Dimensions: Span, 118 ft 7 in (36,15 m); length, 122 ft 10½ in (37,45 m); height, 34 ft 11 in (10,64 m); wing area, 1,529 sq ft (142,0 m²).

Weights: Empty equipped, 82,500 lb (37 422 kg); max payload, 37,000 lb (16 783 kg); max fuel load, 41,130 lb (18 656 kg); max zero fuel, 122,500 lb (55 564 kg); max take-off, 146,500 lb (66 448 kg); max landing, 130,500 lb (61 238 kg).

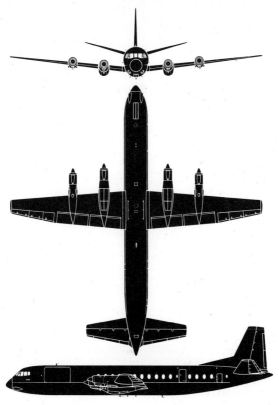

YAKOVLEV YAK-40

Country of Origin: Soviet Union.
Type: Regional airliner.
Power Plant: Three 3,300 lb st (1 500 kgp) Ivchenko AI-25 turbofans.
Performance: Max cruising speed, 342 mph (550 km/h); range with max payload (32 passengers), 900 mls (1 450 km); range with max fuel, 1,118 mls (1 800 km).
Accommodation: Flight crew of two, with provision for third man on flight deck. Standard layout for 27 passengers three-abreast with offset aisle, at pitch of 29.7 in (77,5 cm); maximum high-density seating 32, four abreast at same pitch.
Status: Prototype first flown 21 October 1966. Entered service with Aeroflot 30 September 1968. Production (commercial and military) complete.
Sales: Approximately 1,000 built, principally for use by Aeroflot. Some exports to companies or governments in Italy, Federal Germany, Afghanistan, Angola, Czechoslovakia, Bulgaria, Vietnam, and Yugoslavia.
Notes: Yakovlev's first jet transport, the Yak-40 was designed to meet Soviet needs for a short-haul transport of modest capacity, to replace piston-engined Il-12s and Il-14s, and even older Li-2s. It flies on scheduled services but is also used for ambulance and air taxi duties and several have been supplied for military use. An effort was also made to adapt the Yak-40 for the US commuter airline market, by fitting Garrett TFE731 turbofans and Collins avionics; this programme was handled by ICX Aviation as the X-Avia, but it did not proceed. An all-freight version of the Yak-40 is used in the Soviet Union.

YAKOVLEV YAK-40

Dimensions: Span, 82 ft 0¼ in (25,00 m); length, 66 ft 9½ in (20,36 m); height, 21 ft 4 in (6,50 m); wing area, 735.5 sq ft (70,0 m²).

Weights: Empty weight, 20,725 lb (9 400 kg); max payload, 5,070 lb (2 300 kg); max fuel load, 8,820 lb (4 000 kg); max take-off weight, 35,275 lb (16 000 kg).

YAKOVLEV YAK-42

Country of Origin: Soviet Union.
Type: Short/medium-range jetliner.
Power Plant: Three 14,330 lb st (6 500 kgp) Lotarev D-36 turbofans.
Performance: Max cruising speed, 503 mph (810 km/h) at 25,000 ft (7 600 m); best economy cruise, 466 mph (750 km/h); range with max payload, 560 mls (900 km) at 478 mph (770 km/h) at 29,500 ft (9 000 m); range with payload of 14,330 lb (6 500 kg), 1,864 mls (3 000 km).
Accommodation: Flight crew of two. Standard arrangement for 120 passengers six-abreast with central aisle, at 31.5-in (80-cm) pitch.
Status: First of three prototypes flown 7 March 1975. First production aircraft flown 1980, and Aeroflot services began at the end of that year, on Moscow–Krasnodar route. In production.
Sales: About 50 delivered to Aeroflot by end-1982; of total stated requirement for up to 2,000. First reported export order placed by Aviogenex of Yugoslavia, with deliveries to begin in 1983.
Notes: The Yak-42 is an extrapolation of the Yak-40 design, and is regarded by Aeroflot as one of the most important additions to its fleet, primarily for domestic routes, replacing Tu-134s and other types. First prototype had only 11 deg of sweepback on the wing, increased to 23 deg on later prototypes and production aircraft. The latter also differ from the prototypes in having four-wheel main landing gear bogies in place of twin wheels. Yak-42 services were being introduced only slowly in 1982/83. A "stretched" version to seat 140 passengers is reported under development. .

YAKOVLEV YAK-42

Dimensions: Span, 112 ft 2½ in (34,20 m); length, 119 ft 4¼ in (36,38 m); height, 32 ft 1¾ in (9,80 m); wing area, 1,615 sq ft (150 m²).
Weights: Empty, 63,845 lb (28 960 kg); max payload, 32,000 lb (14 500 kg); max fuel load, 40,785 lb (18 500 kg); max take-off, 117,950 lb (53 500 kg).

INDEX